D0021301

INFERNAL ANGELS

BOOKS BY LOREN D. ESTLEMAN

Kill Zone
Roses Are Dead
Any Man's Death
Motor City Blue
Angel Eyes
The Midnight Man
The Glass Highway
Sugartown
Every Brilliant Eye
Lady Yesterday
Downriver
Silent Thunder
Sweet Women Lie
Never Street
The Witchfinder
The Hours of the
    Virgin
A Smile on the Face of
    the Tiger
City of Widows*
The High Rocks*
Billy Gashade*
Stamping Ground*
Aces & Eights*
Journey of the Dead*
Jitterbug*
Thunder City*

The Rocky Mountain Moving
    Picture Association*
The Master Executioner*
Black Powder, White
    Smoke*
White Desert*
Sinister Heights
Something Borrowed,
    Something Black*
Port Hazard*
Poison Blonde*
Retro*
Little Black Dress*
Nicotine Kiss*
The Undertaker's Wife*
The Adventures of Johnny
    Vermillion*
American Detective*
Gas City*
Frames*
The Branch and the Scaffold*
Alone*
The Book of Murdock*
Roy & Lillie: A Love Story*
The Left-Handed Dollar*
Infernal Angels*

*A Forge Book

INFERNAL ANGELS

An Amos Walker Novel

Loren D. Estleman

A TOM DOHERTY ASSOCIATES BOOK
NEW YORK

INFERNAL ANGELS

Copyright © 2011 by Loren D. Estleman

Edited by James Frenkel

A Forge Book
Published by Tom Doherty Associates, LLC
175 Fifth Avenue
New York, NY 10010

www.tor-forge.com

Forge® is a registered trademark of Tom Doherty Associates, LLC.

Library of Congress Cataloging-in-Publication Data

Estleman, Loren D.
    Infernal angels / Loren D. Estleman.—1st ed.
        p. cm.
    "A Tom Doherty Associates book."
    ISBN 978-0-7653-1955-5
    1. Private investigators—Fiction.   2. Drug traffic—Fiction.   3. Detroit (Mich.)—
Fiction.   I. Title.
    PS3555.S84I64 2011
    813'.54—dc22
                                                                            2011013480
First Edition: July 2011

Printed in the United States of America

0   9   8   7   6   5   4   3   2   1

For Millie Puechner, who was there at the dawn

PART ONE

HIGH DEF IN THE AFTERNOON

ONE

Nothing ever wakes you up from a nightmare, have you noticed?

If you're dreaming of eating strawberries or cutting a ceremonial ribbon or dining with Julia Roberts, you can depend on the alarm or the telephone or a hand on your shoulder to bust in before the payoff, but if your teeth are falling out or a grizzly is charging you, you're in for the duration.

For a week I'd been chasing a car with a car chasing me, and then someone miscued and we all smashed up with me in the middle. I heard rubber howl and metal scream and the squishy crunch of bones breaking and when I woke up I tasted blood.

The latest collision was the same as all the rest. I came out of it with my leg hurting, a low-grade ache that would turn into hours of teeth-grinding agony if I didn't catch it early. I took two Vicodin, chewing them to streamline their way into my circulatory system. The leg always lets me know when a solstice is coming. If you'd rather get that from a calendar, duck the next time someone shoots at you.

There was no sleep until the pills kicked in, and then only the same nightmare. I went into the kitchen, but there wasn't enough coffee left in the can to open one eye.

It was a little short of four A.M. I pulled on a sweatshirt, mildewing jeans from the hamper, and a pair of sneakers, fired up the four-barrel, and drove between canals of dead leaves, crossing intersections where the signals blinked yellow. Away out in space the aircraft warning light on top of the Penobscot Building pulsed on and off, as distant as the Big Dipper. On one corner a man dressed exactly as I was sat on the curb among his duffels and tattered trash bags, eating something from a greasy paper cupped in both hands. He appeared to own more things than I did. These are the thoughts you think at that hour. They can't be healthy.

A few corners down from there a Walgreen's sat in a fluorescent blaze with a handful of cars drifted up against the building. I slid in beside a handicap space, passed through the sliding door, and heard my first Christmas carol of the year on the PA. It was late October and the center aisles were crowded with Halloween costumes and talking skulls.

An orange electric cord snaked between displays of candied peanuts and Trojans, at the end of which a man in blue coveralls was pushing a floor buffer as slowly as if he were sifting for land mines. I walked around him and turned the corner toward the pantry section. The midnight blue uniform of a Detroit patrol officer caught my eye by the tail. He was standing near the pharmacy counter with his back to the rest of the room, staring up at the convex mirror mounted in the corner near the ceiling. The attenuated reflections of the scattered customers slid across the surface, but he didn't appear to be interested in the ones that were moving. He was focused on a skinny figure with his hands buried in the pockets of a hooded gray sweatshirt standing behind a woman being waited on at the counter near the door.

The cop was very big, very black, and I'd had business with him in the past, mostly of the friendly kind. His name was Sergeant Mansanard, but he'd been a detective lieutenant when we'd first met, which was too close to get to the chief when the administration changed. Now he pushed a cruiser through some of the city's worst neighborhoods, frequently without a partner because the mayor had had to cough up a nine-million-dollar settlement for unlawfully terminating a number of Mansanard's fellow officers for taking their oath too literally, and that had led to layoffs.

"You look like you was shit by a pigeon." He didn't glance away from the mirror. He'd probably seen me coming all the way from the parking lot.

"That's good," I said. "Can I use it?"

"Ask my watch captain. I got it from him."

I joined him in the stakeout. We didn't talk police business because voices carried among all those reflective surfaces.

The scrawny kid, if that's what he was, put in a workout just standing there, twitching his shoulders and rolling his head on his neck and flexing his fists in his pockets. They opened onto a pouch that went across the front of his sweatshirt. It wasn't long enough for a sawed-off shotgun, but pistols and revolvers come in all sizes. The woman in front of him, twice as broad in a red coat with a monkey collar, had heaped a stack of men's shirts on plastic hangers on the counter and the clerk went through them one by one, scanning the tags and removing the hangers. I'd have fidgeted, too, but the weather was too mild to pull your hood up over your ears; that's like a cloak of invisibility where surveillance cameras are concerned.

I was starting to feel sorry I'd left the .38 at home. Coffee prices weren't so high I'd figured I'd need it.

At length the woman in the coat wrote out a check and the clerk processed it through his machine and stuffed the shirts in a plastic bag and Gray Hood stepped up and asked for a box of Marlboros. His tone fell somewhere between a mumble and silence. When the clerk asked for ID he took both hands out of his pockets. Mansanard's thumb slid over the blunt hammer of the Beretta in his holster.

The pouch collapsed without support. The clerk peered at the driver's license in the customer's wallet and took a box off a shelf behind him.

Mansanard relaxed, but I stayed tense until money changed hands and the kid left.

"He might've implied he had a weapon," I said.

"That only works in banks. I wish I had more banks on my beat. Clerk's Korean. If he don't have a mag at least under that counter his people would cast him out. We'll just wait a bit. He might've been casing the place."

"After showing ID?"

"If it wasn't fake, maybe he don't plan to leave the clerk in shape to remember it."

Three minutes went by, and one transaction. They seemed longer. The sergeant turned my way with a grin. "That's like a half hour in perp time," he said. "They don't have the attention span to follow a pie fight. Looks like the republic's safe for a little longer. How are you, Amos, still reading room registers?"

"There's no money in that in a no-fault divorce state." I shook his hand. It could have wrapped twice around mine, a white pig in a black blanket, but the grip was barely there. The really big dogs hardly ever feel the need to show their teeth. "They got you on drugstore detail now?"

"Oh, hell, no. I just come in for a juice box. Funny, I thought about calling you tonight."

"No boxes, sorry. I drink straight from the bottle."

"This is work, maybe the paying kind." He looked around. "Care to sit in the cruiser? These places give me the willies, especially at night. All the bad guys are out there in the dark and here you and me sit like a couple of Big Macs under a heat bulb."

"I didn't see a cruiser out front."

"I parked out front, the scroats would just go to the next place down the road and stick it up. Might as well make myself useful."

"Miss C.I.D.?"

"A little, now they're moving out of that dump downtown. I still got mold in my lungs." He coughed into his fist by way of demonstration; something rattled deep in his chest. "I *don't* miss timing my trips to the can so's I don't run into the chief. Now when nature calls I just radio it in and stop at a party store. Let's go out and sit in the bucket."

"As long as my friends don't see me."

"What friends you got, what're the odds?"

We made our purchases and walked around the building to where he'd left his black-and-gold unit next to a Dumpster. Inside, the equipment jammed between the front seats crowded us against the doors: onboard computer, two-way radio, fax machine, piano bar. The winking green and red and amber lights cast his face in opalescent glow, piling shadows under the stony ridge of his forehead and in the hollow of his chin. When he pierced his box of grapefruit juice with a plastic straw and drew on it, the sides caved in and the corners of his police-issue moustache nearly touched. "What you taking for the leg, Demerol?"

"Vicodin. I didn't think I'd limped."

"You was trying too hard not to. I take Demerol for the back. They never will learn how to design these seats for no eight-hour tour." He slurp-slurped. "I'd hate to have to bust you some night for possession."

"So far it's legal. I've got an understanding doctor."

"That's what the suburbs are for. Working late?"

"Not working lately. Business picks up around Devil's Night."

"Mine, too."

"Teenage runaways, mine. All you've got to worry about's vandalism and arson."

"Scraphounds now, too. Strip the copper plumbing out of empty houses, pry up manhole covers, snatch bronze angels from cemeteries and sell 'em to salvage yards. Dig the fillings out of your teeth if you pass out at a bus stop. Whole city's got a bad case of metal-eating termites. If they could get to the suspension cables on the Ambassador Bridge we'd have to swim to Canada."

"There's always the tunnel."

"I'll take my chances in the water, not under it."

I drummed my fingers on the top of the coffee can in the plastic bag in my lap. "Scavengers, is that the job?"

"That's *my* job. Man can gripe, can't he?" He took a business card out of a pocket of his leather tunic and held it out between his first and second fingers.

I took it. It was glossy red with gold letters. I had to turn it this way and that in the reading light to cut the glare. Mansanard siphoned grapefruit juice as I read.

PAST PRESENCE
"Everything you require
for the Modern Regressive Lifestyle"
R. Crossgrain, Prop.

I turned it over. The back was blank. It was as spare as mine: no fax, cell, Web site, e-mail; just the street address and a landline. It was a collector's item. "What's the modern regressive lifestyle?"

"I ain't just sure, but I think you're living it."

I got the rest of what I needed and then his straw gurgled and he crumpled the box in one fist and drove around to my car to save wear and tear on the leg, dropping the box in a curbside container on the way. I thanked him and we separated. Driving away I couldn't shake the feeling I was still dreaming and heading toward that same triple smashup I'd been dreaming about for a week.

I never got the chance to tell Sergeant Mansanard what came of his tip. Four months later, on a mission to buy something flimsy for his wife for Valentine's Day, he walked in on an armed robbery in the Victoria's Secret store in the Fairlane Mall in Dearborn and took a slug through the heart before he could get to his holster.

TWO

arcus Street didn't feature often in the news. So far no meth labs had turned up there and it wasn't one of those neighborhoods where body bags came and went as regularly as rain in Brazil. The address was spelled out in script on the wooden front porch of a narrow brick house in a row of them, with a driveway it shared with the neighbor next door and a TV antenna shaped like an airplane on the roof. Someone had taped a square of cardboard over a broken pane in the front door. I figured that was where the burglar had gained entry.

A tall man with an egg-shaped head opened the door at my knock. He wore a burnt-orange cardigan over a white bowling shirt and shapeless slacks the color of anything. An aluminum baseball bat rested on his left shoulder.

"You want to keep that down around hip level," I said. "Shove it hard into their belly. Swinging takes too much space." I held up my ID folder.

His eyes moved slowly behind rimless glasses, reading the credentials. "Is that badge real?"

"County phased out the design ten or twelve years ago. You can check out the rest with the state police in Lansing."

"I did, right after you called. Your license is up for renewal in December, Mr. Walker."

"I haven't decided yet whether to apply. You're Mr. Crossgrain?"

He nodded, taking inventory. I'd caught a couple of hours' sleep—without dreams—and turned out scrubbed and shaved in a new suit. I seemed to pass inspection, because he stooped to lean the bat against the inside of the door frame and shuffled out of my way in slippers that left his heels bare. He closed and locked the door behind me and led me past a living room full of furniture draped in transparent plastic down a short hallway into a kitchen.

"Will you have a cup of coffee? I'm sorry if I was rude. I didn't get much sleep last night."

"I'd like one, thanks. I bet you slept sitting up with that bat across your lap."

"It was horrible. I've never been broken into before. It's a violated feeling. What do you take in it?" He unplugged a percolator shaped like a spaceship and started pouring.

"Just more coffee." I looked around. "I grew up in a room just like this."

The kitchen was large, built back when everyone in the house gathered there, painted bright green and yellow, with a fluorescent halo ceiling fixture, a laminated table with matching chairs, and a Westinghouse refrigerator with old-fashioned coils on top. An old-fashioned gas range with one of those handles you pumped to bring up the pressure squatted on curved cast-iron legs at the end of a Formica counter.

"The stove and fridge were probably before your time. It's

over the top, I suppose, but you should've seen the place when I moved in. The seventies have a lot to answer for when it comes to architectural vandalism. Renovating it is how I got started."

I accepted a steaming cup, white with a green stripe and as thick as my finger, and we sat down at the table. I watched him doctor his cup with sugar from a kind of dispenser I hadn't seen in years. "So this is what you sell?"

He smiled. He was a year or two older than I was, with grayish skin that looked as if it would preserve thumbprints like putty. His teeth stood out white against it. "Just what part of 'Past Presence' didn't you understand?"

"Sergeant Mansanard told me a little. I figured you could fill in the blanks." Crossgrain's place had been his first radio call of the midnight-to-eight tour.

"He wasn't very encouraging. He wrote down what was missing, with a description, said if anyone tried to sell it and someone saw the stuff on the hot list or otherwise got suspicious the police might recover some of it. He didn't even dust for fingerprints. Is that what they do now, just keep records of crimes for the statistics?"

"The cops solve most crimes. Forensics' pretty strung out. Burglary falls below the middle on the list of priorities. It'd be different if you'd managed to get murdered."

"Is that supposed to be funny?"

"Apparently not." I drank. The coffee tasted heavily of aluminum, but that might have been the power of suggestion based on the Buck Rogers percolator. "It helps to keep things in perspective. Getting ripped off isn't as bad as it can get. I understand you weren't home at the time."

"I got in late from a show in Chicago: Mid-twentieth-century collectibles. It was dark and I hadn't left the porch light on—purposely, to avoid attracting burglars." The smile now was bitter. "I didn't notice the pane was broken until I opened the door and stepped on the glass."

"Dead bolt's not much good when there's a window within reach of the knob. Is this where you do business?"

"From the basement, by appointment. I used to have a shop in Sterling Heights, but I lost my lease when the casinos went in here in town. All that new revenue was going to trickle down to the suburbs, you see. An upscale restaurant stood to pay more rent than a broken-down curiosity shop."

"What was taken?"

He sipped from his cup. He'd kept the spoon in it and braced the handle with his thumb to keep from poking himself in the eye. The gesture reminded me of my father, in a kitchen much like his. "How much do you know about high-definition television?"

"I know I can't afford one."

"Many can't, but they're going to have to scrape up the money soon if they don't want to abandon their reality shows. By federal law, every station in the country is switching to a high-def frequency. That's the end of analog broadcasting. If you have a regular cathode-ray set like we've had since the dawn of television, you won't get a signal."

"You'd think Washington had enough to keep it busy without that."

"The *excuse* is the government wants to reserve the analog frequency for emergency transmissions in the interest of national security, but some of us suspect the flow of campaign money from the manufacturers of plasma and liquid-crystal television receivers helped nudge undecided legislators off the fence. The home electronics industry stands to make trillions—not billions; *trillions*—from that decision over the next ten years."

"Not to mention give aid and comfort to enemy extraterrestials."

He stirred his coffee with deep concentration. "I'm a small businessman, not a conspiracy nut. If I went around lining hats with Alcoa wrap I wouldn't have any time left to balance my books. But even an idiot might ask what's to prevent a terrorist from getting hold of a 1965 Curtis Mathes and tuning in to the latest from NORAD."

"Can we start with your situation, and work our way up to the Pentagon?" I was starting to think the morning was wasted, and I had a lot more of those than dollars.

"Sorry. I'm a little paranoid today. Somebody broke my stuff and made off with some of my other stuff. That's the stuff I'm getting around to. I wasn't quite accurate when I said you couldn't watch HDTV on an analog set. I sell a type of converter box that unscrambles the transmission. It won't deliver HD quality, but it allows you to watch anything broadcast over the new frequency at a fraction of the cost of updating your existing equipment. That's what's missing."

"They stole a converter box?"

"They stole twenty-five, the entire shipment I took delivery on last week. They were still in the shipping boxes."

"What are they worth?"

"Fifty apiece, wholesale. I'd planned to sell them for seventy-five."

I'd gotten most of this from Mansanard, but raw data only, and he hadn't seemed to have grasped the concept of just what had been stolen. If politics hadn't knocked him out of the Criminal Investigation Division, his lack of imagination would have sooner or later.

The loss came to just under nineteen hundred, less than four hundred over my standard retainer for any job that looked as if it would take longer than a day. "A fifty percent markup seems low for retail."

"It was going to be a come-on: Buy an analog set and I'd throw in the converter for seventy-five. A hundred for the box alone."

"Extended warranty?"

"Of course."

The morning was looking up. "Have you got a picture of one or something so I'd know what I was looking for?"

"I'll show you one in person. I bought it to try out before I took the plunge."

We left our cups behind and I followed him through a door and down a flight of plain wooden steps in a narrow well that smelled like potatoes. The place had been a Michigan basement at one time—meaning a hole in the ground with a house on top of it—and no matter how you finish one of those and what kind of equipment you install to change the air you can't quite get rid of that homely funk. I'd never liked it since the day my mother sent me to the potato bin for a big baker and I grabbed a live rat.

At the bottom, Crossgrain palmed up a row of wall switches. There was a pause, then four rows of fluorescent tubes in ceiling troughs fluttered on, pouring icy light into a room the length and width of the house. Three oak timbers supported a massive beam that prevented the first and second floors from collapsing into the basement, where aisles invited visitors to inspect the inventory: vintage suits and dresses on pipe racks, incomplete sets of furniture, radios encased in walnut and Bakelite, bolts of curtain material, curved steel toasters, squat oil burners, wallpaper in rolls, men's and women's hats on Styrofoam heads, cartons of flatware, portable record players, and two rows of TV sets with tiny picture tubes in big oiled-wood cabinets with speakers covered in gold cloth. The twentieth century was having a rummage sale.

Everything was arranged more or less neatly, some of it in stacks that would have to be dismantled to get to the items on the bottom. Here the fetor broke down into a compost of mildew and dry rot, old furniture polish and the unique stench of scorched electrical insulation.

Crossgrain turned off a loudly whooshing dehumidifier. The room fell silent except for the insect buzz of a faulty light fixture. I said, "People buy this stuff, I guess."

"Can't get their fill. I've got a customer who drops in at least twice a week, which is ten times more often than I make significant changes in the stock. Once he bought a whole bedroom suite, birch and bird's-eye maple. Some days he leaves with just a spoon. He's as gay as a bishop, but heteros are just as hot to make a fetish of the past. Every time Bill Gates or Steve Jobs announces a new iPod, I get a flood of orders for steel phonograph needles. Here." He lifted a black rotary telephone off a dusty plant stand. "Two years ago I couldn't give these away. Now I've got a waiting list. The sheer therapeutic pleasure of actually *dialing* a number—even if that number belongs to a cell phone—can be as relaxing as a day in a hot tub."

"Until you run into an electronic menu on the receiving end."

"Then I sell them one of these." He put down the telephone

and slid a gizmo smaller than a cigarette pack from the pocket of his bowling shirt, turning it to show me a keypad on one side and a tiny speaker on the other. "You hold it to the mouth-piece and press the buttons, just like on a touch-tone."

"The simple life's getting more complicated by the day."

"Sometimes the shortest distance between two points is a trip around the barn."

Breaking that one down and combing through it for sense took too much time. "Anything else missing?"

"No. They seemed to know just what they wanted."

"Who knew you had them?"

"I told some people at the Chicago show, but don't ask me who. I didn't get the name of everyone I met there. I ordered them through an eight-hundred number. That's not exactly a secure line, but it beats using the Internet." He scampered two aisles over and trotted back carrying something metal and rectangular from the TV section. For a tall man he moved around like a fighting cock.

The box was the size of a desk humidor, lighter than it looked. It had a power button, no other controls, and two ports in back for plugging in cables. A copper plate on the back contained a twelve-digit serial number and the name "MacArthur Industries," followed by a post office box in Southfield. Just then the name meant nothing to me, but time had passed and I'd either forgotten or blocked it out. It brought no chills.

THREE

I never made five hundred dollars on my best day," Crossgrain said.

"What about the bedroom suite you sold the bishop?"

"I said he was as *gay* as a bishop. He's a landscape architect. Okay, I guess that would be my best day. That was two years ago. Can you guarantee you'll recover my merchandise so I can earn it back?"

"What guarantee did you get from the cops?"

"They're paid either way."

"So am I, but you get my whole day for the price." I gave him back his box. "Three days in advance, for wear and tear."

His egg-shaped head flushed from crown to chin. "I don't figure to make much more than that from the lot. What *kind* of wear and tear?"

"Tires, long-distance bills, cranial surgery. I don't expect the trail to lead to the Grosse Pointe Yacht Club."

He turned his attention to the row of Admirals, Dumonts, Tele Kings, and a Philco that shared a monster blonde cabinet the shape and size of a coffin with an AM radio and a three-speed record changer: space-eaters all, without a converter to pick up a signal. Ten minutes later, back on the ground floor, he came out of a den off the hallway waving a check to dry the ink from a fountain pen. I wondered if he'd worn sleeve protectors while he was drawing it up. He held it back, leaving my hand flapping. "What if the police recover my property before the three days are up?"

"You get back what I don't spend."

He gave me the check then. I frowned at the signature. "Is Crossgrain your real name?"

"I get that a lot. Yes, it is. I don't pretend it wasn't an influence."

I put away the check and said I'd report. Making me grab air the first time was going to cost him, but he didn't have to know that.

I put a thousand in savings and held out the rest for graft. Some of it went to a pawnbroker on Willis who had a clean ticket downtown because he reported everything from the hot sheet that showed up on his counter, or enough anyway to fill suspicious silences. He wouldn't touch a shoplifted watch or a Turkish rug that had vanished from a house in Birmingham, but if the price was right he'd direct whoever came in with it to the fence that would give him the best deal. Several search warrants had failed to turn up an incriminating piece of evidence because he kept all the merchandise in his head. He'd put a daughter through Princeton and his son was at Annapolis. Neither had spoken to him in years.

The place was built like a bank, as most things are in a town where even the sidewalk Santas go heeled. The cash lay untouched in the sliding steel tray while his eyes scanned my retinas through bulletproof Plexiglas. He was a West Indian, with dreads and a set of those chin whiskers you could scrape off with a thumbnail.

We'd been through this before. I said, "Where'll I go to-morrow if I roll over on you today?"

"Once is all it takes."

I made a move to retrieve the bills. I almost lost fingers. The tray banged in and back out empty, a magic act.

"'Lectronics is a big field." Thirty years in Detroit had erased the island from his speech.

"Give me three names to start, off the top."

"Bud Lite."

"Real names."

"I don't know the real one. That was his hip-hop tag till he washed out."

"I didn't know you could."

"Felony murder."

"Is that a prior or the name of another rap artist?"

"This one stuck. Through the preliminary, anyway. He's out on a million dollars' bail, but the corpse belonged to the owner of a record label, so he isn't in show business anymore. He runs a storefront op uptown, dealing hot components to pay his lawyer."

"I must've been away on vacation when that story broke. Except I haven't had a vacation in twenty years."

"It went down in the corpse's house in Guam, same day they hanged Saddam Hussein. I think it ran after the weather."

"Which storefront?"

He gave me an address from memory. I repeated it, committing it to memory. I'd sooner have drawn a pistol there than a notebook. He kept a fowling piece under the counter.

"Johnny Toledo."

These were actual names. I don't make them up.

I shook my head. "I know Johnny. Scavenging's his lay." He was one of those scraphounds Sergeant Mansanard had been griping about.

"He's diversified since the accident. Second-story windows aren't wheelchair accessible."

"Still in the same place?"

"Till they knock it down."

"Who's left?"

"Eugenia Pappas."

"Eugenia, how'd a Eugenia get in there?"

A buzzer announced a customer at the door. He glanced at a monitor connected to a security camera outside and hit the electronic lock. A squat dark party in a Red Wings cap and a dirty quilted jacket inappropriate for a mild day shuffled in trailing a pair of loose shoelaces, hesitated when he saw me, then picked up his pace as I stepped away from the counter. He had something bulky under the jacket.

It turned out to be a toaster oven with the cord wrapped around it. When he set it on the counter, the pawnbroker un-latched and slid the Plexiglas shield to one side and transferred the oven to a shelf on his side. He peeled two bills off a roll he took from his pocket. The money disappeared inside the dirty jacket and the man scuttled on out.

I reached up and closed my mouth.

The shield slammed back into place with a savage jerk. "Mr. Walters from down the street. Still paying for his wife's funeral. His apartment must be pretty empty by now. What's that last thing you said?"

"Eugenia."

"Nick Pappas' widow. He sold the first stolen eight-track player in Michigan. His old man hijacked truckloads of TVs in forty-eight. His grandfather smuggled crystal sets into the U.S. piece by piece in the assholes of German POWs during World War One. Nick didn't have any kids of his own, so Eugenia's carrying on the family business."

"She's practically legitimate."

"She's fucking royalty, and you better treat her that way if you don't want to wind up picking asphalt out of your teeth."

Her address was on a residential street I knew in St. Clair, bang on the river within spitting distance of Ontario, Canada; although no one who lived there ever spat unless he got a mouthful of bad beluga. I'd told Crossgrain wrong. I hadn't expected a simple smash-and-grab affair to lead anywhere that close to the silk.

"I'll be back if those don't pan out."

"Your client's got deep pockets."

"Paris Hilton deep; her personality, not her purse. It shouldn't cost him another cent. A story like poor Mr. Willis' could draw every sad sack in three stories to your door with a small appliance under his arm."

His face clouded. It doesn't take long for some people to smell blackmail. "You're a son of a bitch."

I felt like one; but I lit a cigarette and waited.

He scratched the pubic patch under his lip. "I gave you the cream. Converter boxes are the latest hot ticket. Bud, Johnny, and Mrs. Pappas are always first in line."

"Okay. How much to redeem the toaster oven?" I took out my wallet.

"Forget it, it's busted. This is the second time I bought it from Willis. He goes through the Dumpster out back."

"Sucker."

"Just for that I'll take your money next time."

St. Clair seemed a good place to start. It was a nice day to drive and I was dressed for the neighborhood.

The sun spanked Anchor Bay hard as I circled the shore, drawing bright rings that stung my eyes even through dark glasses. Dorsal-shaped sails leaned steeply into the wind from the Dominion of Canada. It was a little cold out there for the size of the traffic, but the season was drawing to a close. In a few weeks the blue would turn to white and only the canvas and plastic yurts of ice fishermen would break up the Arctic landscape.

I knew a bit about the Pappases. Alexander, founder of the clan, had taken the experience he'd gained smuggling in crystal sets and invested it in the liquor trade when demand was at its peak. He'd run with the Oakland Sugar House Gang for a spell, then when the largely Jewish Purple Gang took over Detroit and enrolled its children in the highly re-garded Catholic school system in St. Clair Shores, moved his base of operations farther north to establish the first Greek Orthodox Church in St. Clair County. He was also credited, when a subordinate stood trial for murdering a Purple, with importing the Texas Defense to Michigan, winning acquittal on grounds that the victim's death served society's best inter-est. No plaque commemorated either event.

The house was one of those German Bauhaus designs that look as if they started out on separate drawing boards. Everything—windows, doors, the slope of the roof—was off-center, making the stately Cape Cod on either side ap-pear even more orderly by comparison. It was an arrangement of cream-colored brick worn smooth at the corners by seventy years of lashing winds and water, overlooking the channel connecting Lake Huron to the rich man's wading pool of Lake St. Clair, and sized modestly by later standards, six thousand square feet at the outside. No iron horse heads or midget windmills interrupted the clean blue-green sweep of the front lawn. The mailbox at the end of the black asphalt driveway was a duplicate of the house in miniature, with a tiny Greek flag on a pivot.

I parked to the side of a four-car garage and used a knocker fashioned in bronze after Zeus's head. With each generation, it seemed, the Pappases had drifted deeper into their cultural heritage. By all accounts, Alexander had applied for U.S. citizenship as soon as he was eligible and forbade everyone in his household from speaking any language other than English.

Once I'd lifted that knocker I had all I could do to let it fall back against the brass plate. There was still time to lower it gently and skedaddle. It seemed I'd spent my life in the company of gangsters and their children and their grandchildren's widows, and the conversation was always the same: stalls, threats, and warnings, sometimes naked, sometimes buttered with the watery margarine of store-bought culture, but always to the same point. The family lines of Washington and Shakespeare had played out, but the boys in silk undies seemed never to run short of seed, and whatever the combination was of chromosomes and conditioning that had made them what they were in the beginning, it passed from father to child and from spouse to spouse like the family silver. I'd begun to feel like the tradesman to a specific kind of royalty, with permission to use the coat-of-arms in my Yellow Pages ad: a tommy gun rampant on a field of cement overcoats. I could apply for a pension any time, if they paid off in cash instead of dum-dums.

What-ho, and all that pother. I let the striker fall, and gave it two more for good measure. I had an appointment.

A woman in a herringbone business suit found out who I was and let me in. Nick had left his first wife for a kitten from a fresh litter, but this one was too young even for that; I figured her for Eugenia's personal assistant. She had cranberry hair, bobbed with bangs, and a little too much going on about the waist and calves, but that could have been protective plumage to get her through the beauty wars alive. She left me in the entryway with some porcelain blobs on glass shelves and came back a minute later to say Mrs. Pappas would receive me in the morning room.

This was a lopsided den on the east side of the house with heavy mesh curtains drawn against the strong sunlight and a lot of functional furniture, including a Prairie style desk made of blanched plywood. Here the mistress of the house sat on a stool shuffling through a stack of mail with a pair of glasses straddling her nose in graphite rims.

It was the same nose they chiseled out of marble two thousand years ago, straight and bold, with a tall planed forehead resting on the bridge and just enough flesh on the rest to prevent bone from poking through. She wore her hair—blonde with a silver wash—pulled straight back into a knot at the base of her skull. The swiftly moving hands were long and thin and blue-veined. She sat in an upright starter's position, hip-shot, with the muscles in her long thighs tense under a thin wool dress, toes braced in open shoes with low platforms. A handsome woman, to use the gentleman's term, built along engineering lines; a utility piece, like the furniture.

"Beggars all." She drummed the unopened envelopes together and laid them on the desk off-center, in keeping with the house. "I'm on the board of several charitable foundations. That means the hoboes' sign is on my gate. Sit, Mr. Walker. The seats are more comfortable than they look."

I gave my one eighty-five to a square black leather chair with a chromium frame. "I came to ask about the supply side." I told her what I was after. I'd run out of small talk for her type and her type's type.

"I'm hopelessly twentieth century. I had a cell phone, but lost it, and I gave away the Palm Pilot someone gave me. There's one computer in the house, in Ouida's office. You met Ouida just now. I'm afraid I wouldn't know a converter box if I saw one."

"Your late husband built this house oh bootleg electronics. I'm not working for the authorities, Mrs. Pappas. If I were I wouldn't waste a visit calling you a footpad. Those boxes have to be moved through someone and your shop's the biggest around."

"I sold all Nick's interests to his competitors after he died. You should speak to them."

"I heard you kept a toe in."

"I never had one in to begin with." She folded her glasses and tapped them against her teeth, small teeth and bright. "I can circulate the word, of course. Nick was highly respected in his field and some of his old friends stay in touch. What kind of incentive are you offering?"

"Freedom from incarceration."

"Life isn't Monopoly. I doubt whoever stole the merchandise gave much thought to the possibility of arrest."

I stood. "I'll find the stuff. The longer it takes and the harder I have to work for it, the smaller the offer."

"For a man with nothing to sell, you're not trying very hard."

"I've got other stops. If you had the plunder piled up in shipping boxes out front I'd stay to make the pitch."

She put the glasses back on and found a steel pencil. "One of the boards I serve on provides counseling to small businesses. I'll do what I can for your client. Who knows? I could be a victim myself one day. Who's the manufacturer?" She turned over an envelope to write on the back. A proper pad would be redundant in her world.

I told her. It still didn't trigger anything for me, but her pencil seemed to hesitate before she wrote the name. The lead might have been brittle.

FOUR

The woman with the cranberry hair was standing in the entryway with her hands folded at her waist. "I just got off the house phone with Mrs. Pappas. If you'll give me all your contact information I'll get back to you with results."

I gave her a card, pointing out the cell number written on the back. "What does being a personal assistant pay these days?"

Her professional smile was unaltered, but now her eyebrows came into play. "Can we start with religion and sex first, and work our way up to my net worth?"

"I'm trying to find out if you can be bribed."

She nodded, considering. "The salary's high by local standards, but I have to be available day and night, and calling in sick isn't an option. I can't expect her to put her life on hold waiting for the antibiotics to kick in."

"So the answer's . . . ?"

"No. Unless you can come up with three months' severance."

"I was thinking dinner."

"What is it you wanted?"

"She says she spends most of her time doing good works. What's she do with the rest of it?"

"You mean, does she meet people in parking lots with a trunkload of MP3s? I hate to crush your hopes, but the answer to that one is also no."

"What would it be if I came up with the three months?"

"The same. She's clean, Mr. Walker. I had some reservations when I applied for the position. Google took me straight to her husband's police file. I came from a small town—"

"Where folks never locked their doors."

She shook her head. "If such places ever existed, they were gone before my time. That doesn't mean I didn't want to make my people proud of me. But I've been here almost two years and she hasn't asked me to do anything so sinister as pay an old parking ticket."

"That should've made you suspicious right off the bat." I looked for a change in her expression, but she'd put it on with the herringbone. "Ouida, where'd that come from?"

"Louisa de la Ramee. She wrote under that name. My mother was on a French novel jag. What about Amos? The Bible?"

"A coin. Andy was on the other side. Mrs. Pappas said she'd ask around. That means you. Do you have to go to her first with what you dig up?"

"Well, it's not in the job description, but it's sort of implied."

"There's some room there I could work a dinner into."

"Listen, mister, I may be fat, but that doesn't mean I'm always hungry. When I am I can feed myself."

I'd gotten the polite smile off her face finally, but I'd had to put my foot in my mouth to do it.

"Working so close to a set of bones like Mrs. Pappas doesn't make you fat," I said. "Does the set of bones ever do business with MacArthur Industries?"

"What did she say?" The question had thrown her off her snit.

"I didn't ask. There's a P.O. box in Southfield, but that's just a drop. It could be in Maine or Manila. I got the impression Mrs. Pappas was familiar with it."

"The impression; I see. It doesn't ring a bell, and I'm in charge of her correspondence."

"She was charging through her own just now."

"She likes to fondle the incoming, after I weed out the junk and items too small to bother her with. Shouldn't you be asking her all these questions?"

"I only asked three, not counting Ouida. That one was for me."

She held up my card like a stop sign. "Wait for my call."

I cleared out. The pawnbroker had warned me I'd be picking asphalt from my teeth if I forgot my manners with Eugenia Pappas, but he hadn't said the bouncer would be named after a French novelist.

The next drip in the pan lived in northwest Detroit, in a house built with federal funds by a late former governor of Michigan who'd been booted one notch above his competency level. There had been dozens of the simple saltboxes, but too much red tape to put tenants in them, so most had been torn down at the city's expense to displace crack dealers. When the demolition money drained away the rest were left to peel and pucker on shaggy lots with barbed wire on either side. In our city of just under a million, the ratio of empty houses to homeless people is about even, with pad-locks separating the one from the other.

Johnny Toledo had left the padlock intact and cut himself a private entrance in the side with a chain saw, leaning the cut-out piece against the hole for privacy. He'd been more mobile then. When I called out his name I heard a trundling noise inside and saw a brown eye peeking around the edge of the hunk of siding. A grunt of invitation followed, then the trundling noise again, receding a couple of yards. A visit from me usually meant cash.

I shoved the obstacle aside and slid it back into place be-hind me Ali Baba style. Johnny poked his boys' model .22 rifle into its scabbard on the side of his wheelchair. "Yo."

"Yo ho ho." I glanced around. "Home sweet scrapyard."

Someone—Johnny, probably, before the accident—had knocked out all the partitions, making the entire ground floor into one room with the bathroom stool exposed and holes in the wall where the kitchen sink and gas appliances had been ripped out by a scavenger who'd gotten there ahead of him and a freestanding staircase leading to the second story he never used. There was no furniture, just a clearing in the piles of coiled copper wire, weeping transmissions, snarls of plumb-ing elbowed into right angles, stacks of twelve-volt batteries, and manhole covers arranged in neat columns like poker chips, with a couple of strays leaned up against them the way some primitive islanders kept their wealth of giant stone coins.

"I ain't just entertaining lately," he said.

He was a fair-skinned black of thirty or so, with an Errol Flynn moustache and a shaved head he covered with a navy knit watch cap in all seasons. His clothes were army surplus:

shapeless camo pants, combat boots, and fatigue shirts with someone else's name stitched above the pocket and sleeves long enough to use for oven mitts.

The wheelchair was stolen, like everything else on the site, including the electricity he used to warm his hot plate, courtesy of a hundred-foot drop cord plugged into an outlet in a crawl space belonging to a clueless neighbor; in winter the plate provided his only heat, and all year around it filled the house with the suety smell of cooking hot dogs, his main staple. In his day Johnny had enjoyed a reputation as a daredevil among salvage thieves, scaling trellises, leaping from roof to roof like Cary Grant, and crawling through storm drains to recover metal to sell to incurious junk dealers. That had ended the night he shinnied up an Edison pole to retrieve a silver conductor and fifty thousand volts flung him fifteen feet to the ground, shattering his spine and paralyzing him below the waist. Now he operated a clearinghouse for his former competitors, receiving scrap at a rate just below the market and reaping the profit from retailers. Located as he was conveniently close to the source of most of the merchandise, he spared his clients the time and risk of transporting truckloads of contraband outside the city limits. His carriers were illegal aliens who thought minimum wage was a democratic myth.

I asked him how business was.

"Sterling." He smiled, showing a gold tooth he'd fashioned by hand from a cable connection. It was the only joke he remembered and it never failed to break the ice.

"I hear you're expanding."

"Yeah, I'm starting a chain. You want a franchise?"

"Electronics is what I heard."

"Too far over the line. Did you know there's no law in this town against swiping fixtures from vacant buildings? Cop catches you in the act, worst he can do's slap you with criminal trespass. I could practically apply for a small bidness loan."

"Moving the fixtures is something else again."

"Priority zero: too many felonies, not enough cops to go around. Swap it for stereos and GPS, all that hot-ticket shit, bar goes way up. Figure in lawyers, bail, loss of work; pound for pound I make ten times more ripping wires and jacks out of busted VCRs in people's trash than I'd get boosting laptops from Best Buy." He had the brain of an accountant. Thieves often do.

"What about converter boxes?"

"What the fuck are them?"

I told him. He touched his wisp of a moustache to make sure it hadn't fluttered away. His smile was tight-lipped. "And here I thought I was missing my MTV. Shit." Gold glinted. "This time next year the country'll be up to its dick in obsolete sets dumped out at the curb. Thousands and thousands of miles of copper and silver wire, aluminum chassis, brass and steel screws. Gonna have to put some more men on the job."

"Glad I could be the bearer of good tidings." Casting about for a fresh tactic I spotted something shiny standing on a folding metal tray from the Eisenhower era, a naked cherub about a foot tall with a twist of wire sticking out of its upraised fist, a sconce intended to perch on a wall shelf. It looked like solid gold or heavy plate, off by itself away from the rest of the inventory. I hadn't noticed it before, but this was the first time I'd dropped in on him since the accident.

He saw my interest. "That come from the old Dodge mansion just before they knocked it down."

"You were in diapers then."

"My old man snuck in through a basement window, right under the nose of a private security patrol: *three times*. That's how many trips it took to get that and some other ornamental shit and about a hundred feet of brass stair rods. I seen it in a pile in a junkyard where I had bidness, dirty as hell, looked like cheap brass. Only piece of salvage I ever paid full price for." Translation: acquired legally. "That was before my spill."

"Your father was a scraphound?"

"Still would be, if he didn't get stuck in a duct in a shut-up factory in Flatrock and die of pneumonia. I used to pretend that thing was my twin brother till the old man sold it. I thought it was melted down twenty years ago."

"If you paid brass prices, it could've helped settle your hospital bill."

"I wouldn't swap it for a new spinal cord. It's all I got to remember the man taught me all I know."

That's why Detroit is never coming back. All the crooks are second- and third-generation.

"Those converter boxes will move fast," I said. "There's a hundred in it if one shows up here and you call me."

"What's one worth?"

"A hundred in the store, but you won't pay twenty."

"That's all you want, the box?"

I lit a cigarette, blew smoke away from him. His lungs wouldn't be in much better shape than his old man's for as much exercise as he got rolling back and forth across that little space of bare floor. "One box won't do my client any good. He lost twenty-five when someone broke in on him. To get the rest I need to find the man. Or the woman."

"Women's got too much sense for that kind of lay. You're

never sure if someone's home, or what he's carrying. He shoots first, you're dead. You shoot first, you get to shower with skin-heads till your pecker dries up and falls off." He shook his head. "I shit in a bag. That's whack. It gets out I gave up a customer's name, somebody comes here and *feeds* me the bag. That's worse."

"Moot point. You don't deal in electronics."

His forehead creased. He'd stumbled over his own lie. "Let's see the hundred."

I folded the bill around a card and gave it to him. Johnny was a fence, not a welsher. And he couldn't run. "Got a phone?"

He produced a clamshell from a flap pocket. "It's a camera too. I gave one to the kid I send for hot dogs so he can send back pictures. I can't make him understand what's wrong with turkey franks." He put it away with the currency and my card.

I went out and put the piece of siding back in place. I didn't know where he kept his cash, but once or twice a year Detroit General Hospital admitted a patient from the neighborhood with a .22 slug in his leg and no satisfactory explanation for how he got it. Johnny was a light sleeper and never left the house.

I'd asked him once if Toledo was his legal name or if he had some connection with the Ohio city on the lake; all he'd said was he'd spent his entire life in Detroit. Half answers were as much as you could expect from him for free.

FIVE

thought I'd make a commando call on Bud Lite in his storefront uptown without letting him know I was coming, but the job needed doping out and I needed to eat first. Inside Johnny Toledo's, the lingering effect of all those scorched wieners was nausea; outside, I was ravenous. I made arrangements at a window for a fish sandwich and a fountain drink, then reported to my private pew in the periodicals section of the library. On the way up the steps I threw some melted ice on top of a couple of Vicodin and dumped the cup in the trash.

Photos of Saddam Hussein before and after his execution filled the front pages and inside sections of both the *News* and *Free Press*, but I found some nutshucks buried inside about the rap musician's arrest in Guam for the fatal shooting of a man named Winfield, who owned a recording label and the house where the shots were fired. Bud Lite's real name was Gale Kreski. He was a native of Hamtramck who ran a music store on the north end of Woodward Avenue, up near where the birds flew in the spring. The story got more play when he was indicted, and posted a hundred thousand dollars' surety on a million dollars' bail, receiving permission to return home while awaiting trial.

The territorial authorities believed the incident had started with a dispute over sales and promotion and finished with three slugs in Winfield's chest as he sat on his terrace overlooking the Pacific. A cropped photo of the dead man with six hands on his shoulders featured the usual bald-headed butterball in an earring and trick spectacles.

People with recording contracts seemed to spend as much time posing for mugs as shooting videos, and I never heard where the bounty had been lifted on executives in the music industry, but the amount some bond company had ponied up to keep Kreski/Lite out of the tank was worth a splash in the media. Counting back the dates I figured out I'd been defending my life in a house in Iroquois Heights at the time, a legitimate distraction. But because most Americans couldn't find the United States Territory of Guam on a map, the story fell like a busted satellite and burned up during descent. Even an album cover shot of the accused pointing a Glock at potential fans couldn't slow it down.

He looked mild enough, despite the ordnance: one of the growing minority of local white hip-hop artists, with long ratty fair hair and a nose as big as a Polish fieldpiece under a porkpie hat, pale eyes with black pupils punched in the centers. A kid with a cap pistol appeared more dangerous.

It seemed he had enough on his plate without receiving and selling stolen goods; but I'd always heard you needed something to fall back on in case you washed out in show business.

I wasn't going on appearances. Back in the car I paid a visit to the gun room and clipped on the .38.

Away from downtown, the scenery along the main stem looks less like part of a big city and more like a series of small towns deserted by an interstate: check-cashing places, two-for-one tattoo stalls, storefront campaign headquarters, mini-marts built like penitentiaries, and a Great Wall of China of plywood and spray paint, the only retail items that have trouble keeping up with the regional demand. The same dusty heirlooms make the rounds of all the pawn shops, all located conveniently next to corner lube joints and the crap games and dog fights inside. I watched a seagull too old to migrate to a choicer neighborhood picking at cracks in the sidewalk behind a walker.

Decade upon decade of weather and monoxide had gnawed the letters clean off the side of the four-story building that housed the music shop, but the darker brick where the paint had been still advertised the name of a hardware store and its date of establishment: 1908. Back then, the city had been known more for kitchen stoves than automobiles, and not at all for the businesses that have faded away with the paint. Sleek Stratocasters beckoned to customers from behind heavy plate-glass windows, with some decorative gravel strewn about to cover the chains shackling them to the superstructure. The entrance was set back in a rectangle made of more glass with a gold decal warning burglars that the place was protected by Reliance Alarm Systems, a division of the biggest detective agency in metropolitan Detroit, which broke out in hives at the very thought of the competition I offered.

The store's name was Felonious Monk Music. The reference was probably lost on most of the clientele, but considering its owner's current circumstances was good for a chuckle. A crude cartoon of a monkey brandishing a switchblade hung from a post above the door, probably to prevent ignorant questions. A jazzy downbeat answered for a bell when I let myself inside.

Nothing much seemed to have been done by way of remodeling since hardware-store days: broad swept planks creaked underfoot and the ceiling was pressed tin. Where kegs of bolts and sacks of washers had stood, more guitars leaned rakishly on stands. Woodwinds and brass suggested a swing band at rest behind the counter and there were the usual racks of picks and reeds and packages of strings and sheet music in pocket racks. A life-size cutout of Bruce Springsteen, made from the same sturdy cardboard used to make the original, drew attention to a display of DVDs that promised to teach guitar virtuosity in ten easy steps. Posters of pop icons all around and a bare spot of floor where something had stood that was heavy enough to make three distinct impressions in the solid pine planks.

"Eggshell-finish Yamaha baby grand. When it went, I cried more than when my grandma died, and she raised me from age two."

This was a good voice, resonant without being self-aware, with the promise of more in reserve. It belonged to a man who'd come in from the back and stood at the end of the showcase counter wiping his hands with a streaked chamois cloth. I caught a strong whiff of 3-in-1 Oil, a not unpleasant tang that took me back to seventh-grade band, third chair; cornet valves will stick if you don't lubricate them regularly.

No Glock, no porkpie hat, and he'd tied his ragged locks into a meager ponytail behind his neck, but he looked enough like his album cover not to fool a determined autograph hound or a border guard with basic training. He photographed older, and his eyes in person were not so much pale as the bright artificial blue of pool chalk: tinted contact lenses, possibly, although I figured him more likely these days to avoid attention rather than seek it out.

"I'm guessing it went toward bail," I said. "A fine instrument like that's worth more in draw than a flat-out sale."

He went on kneading the cloth. He had on a plain black T-shirt and Levi's that looked as if they'd worn honestly; torn at the crotch, not at the knees, uneven frays at the cuffs, a broad square lick from a brush loaded with whitewash. The brand of jeans belonged to an earlier generation, the inventor of hip, now solidly mainstream. His bare arms were a blue smear of elaborate needlework, each design screaming for attention in a mob.

He said, "I'm innocent. That's the party line, on orders from my lawyer. You're the third person today came in to look at me instead of the stock. I guess I'm the piano now."

"Maybe I came for the stock."

"You look like a musician," he said, "like I look like a cop. What's your pleasure?"

"It's not as bad as that." I showed him my ID with the deputy's badge folded out of sight; he'd seen enough of those lately.

He folded the cloth into a neat square and laid it on the counter. His biceps were lean and moved smoothly under the ink-stained skin. I guessed martial-arts training, and wondered how many moves I remembered. "I guess everyone has a family, even a rat like Winfield. Ask your clients what they'd do if somebody promised you five million dollars, withheld ninety percent pending returns, and cut you off after one album on a three-album deal."

"Go on a five-hundred-thousand-dollar drunk. But that's just me."

"What if you spent every cent on a house for your parents, a place in Grosse Pointe for yourself, this dump for the tax write-off, a fat salary for your publicist, and loans to all the friends who promised to pay you back with interest, only you said, no, no, pay me back what I lent you when you can, but they never paid back even that?"

"Go on a cheaper drunk. Old Milwaukee instead of Grey Goose. I'd still have the piano." I put away the credentials. "I'm not investigating what went down in Guam. I'm tracking a shipment of stolen HDTV converters. They walked out of a house in Detroit sometime over the weekend."

"Oh, Christ. Bait a second hook in case I slip off the first. I didn't kill anyone and I don't deal in electronics, stolen or otherwise."

"No one in town deals in them. I asked. I'm starting to think it's all outsourced to China."

"Mister, I'm looking at fifty to life in a Philippine shithole for improper disposal of an earring with a piece of shit attached to it. Turning fence wouldn't cozy me up to the jury."

"The scatology's sound, but the reasoning's shaky. You're into a bailbondsman for a hundred grand and you've got a lawyer to feed. If I were in your position I'd sell anything I could get my hands on."

"Including your good name?"

"Which one. Gale Kreski or Bud Lite?"

"One's easier to spell and download." He scratched a tattoo and looked at his nails to see if it had come off. He'd lost his faith in every transaction. "My great-grandfather came through Ellis Island with a cardboard suitcase and fifty zlotys sewed inside the lining of his coat. That was about ten dollars American. He came to Detroit and hammered out engine blocks at Dodge. Thirty-six years of that and then an artery blew out in his brain right at the end of his shift. Two hundred people went to his funeral in St. Stanislaus', counting friends and four dozen relatives he helped bring over from the Old Country. I never knew him, but my grandma told me stories every day, each one more saintly than the last. *No*body's that good, but I wouldn't turn thief and piss on his grave."

"Where'd he stand on murder?"

His skin was fair and flushed at the first sign of rain, but that was as far as it went. "I told you twice I'm innocent."

"How about Great-Grandpa? I thought all you Polacks had a dead Cossack in the family closet."

That worked. I'd begun to think nothing would. He was fast, and I had twenty years on him, hard ones with painkillers crawling through my veins, but rock beats scissors. I cleared the .38 just as his right foot left the floor.

It was a near thing even then. The two yards that separated us spared me a bad case of athlete's chin. He caught himself in mid-kick and lowered the foot.

"I wish I *had* killed the son of a bitch." He was breathing hard. "If I had, I'd do the time satisfied."

"People say that who never did time. But I believe you. If I didn't before, I do now. You'd have kicked him off his terrace, not shot him. I don't buy you on that album cover. No wonder it didn't sell. You forgot to take off the safety."

"I let Winfield talk me into posing for it. It was wrong on every level. I told him I'm no gangsta, but he said if I expected people to believe that I should tell them I came from Wichita. He seriously thought 'Detroit iron' meant guns."

"He should've dumped the campaign and run with Ellis Island. I don't think anyone's ever shot a video there, but I've lost touch. My cable went out."

"White Stripes, last year." His smile was lost in the shade of the strong Balkan nose. "I opened for them in Cleveland."

"Who killed him?" I don't know why I asked. Every case doesn't have to lead to murder.

"Record producers make child pornographers look like Bambi, and Winfield made other record producers look like Saint fucking Joan. He hired armed Chamorro to patrol his grounds day and night because of all the death threats he got. My guess? Somebody paid one of his Chamorro to cap him, ten minutes after I left his place. We were yelling loud enough to be heard in American Samoa."

"No wonder they call it rap."

The smile stuck. "Ever investigate homicide?"

"Not in Guam."

"I couldn't afford it anyway. Converters, you said?"

I nodded; realized I was still holding the revolver and returned it to its clip. "Twenty-five of them, still in boxes. They're all that was taken, so the burglars knew what they were after. They'll try to unload the shipment in a lump. Piecing it out takes too long and burns gas."

"Price at the pump affects everything, even larceny. I'm told. I haven't seen 'em, but like I said."

Not being a fence was the part of his story I didn't believe, but life's too short to argue with a black belt. "They might try to move them through a music shop, to throw off the cops. You didn't ask what converters are, so the businesses must overlap." I put a card on a padded stand supporting an arrangement of amplifiers on different levels. "My cell's on the back. I can throw a hundred or so into your defense fund if the sellers show up and you can keep them around."

"A hundred'd buy a half-hour with my counselor."

"That's the job. It isn't a big job as jobs go, but they don't fall off overpasses like chunks of concrete. The governor says we're in a one-state recession."

"How about something on account?"

"Sorry. A judge could revoke your bail any time and whisk you off to that shithole in the Philippines."

"I can make a lot more off the converters themselves. If I were in the racket."

"I'd find out. I wouldn't make a good character witness at your trial."

He flushed again. I let myself out, elaborately in no hurry. Back on the street I resumed breathing. My quick-draw is only good for one charge.

SIX

My walk-in trade had stood still since *Saw II*, but I swung by the office to throw away my mail on the way home. That was two flights of stairs too many for the leg. Back in the house I left the pills alone and fixed myself some old-school relief from the vintage in the kitchen cupboard. It wouldn't win me any marathons but it would hold me until bedtime and the next round of vehicular nightmares.

I played with my Scotch and watched the local stations run ten minutes of news on a loop for an hour and a half. There were more fatal drug overdoses around town than usual, I thought, but being a borderline addict myself maybe I was just more sensitive to it. Even so, on the evidence, some souped-up grade of heroin from Asia or the Middle East was blasting its way through a network more accustomed to friendly old Mexican brown. Every twenty years or so these things swept in like an Alberta Clipper, clearing out the shelters and rehab clinics, then moved on to wealthier markets in Hollywood and D.C. Somewhere along the line the city had become a testing laboratory for new product.

Reuben Crossgrain, my client, got his fifteen seconds between spots for a burger chain and a treatment for hemorrhoids whose side effects included cholera. The only reason his B and E got any air at all was it allowed a consumer affairs reporter to lead into a canned feature about truckloads of analog TVs rolling into landfills: Another great day for planet Earth.

Crossgrain showed off his sample box and managed to get the name Past Presence into the sound bite. I made a mental note to hit him up for another advance when the three days were up, based on the business it brought in. If he'd mentioned me at all it was lost in editing.

If my profit margin were wider than a worm's whisker I'd offer the first day free. It's almost always squandered on leads that don't lead and tips that don't tip. I'd made practice casts over two counties and pulled up a pawnbroker with a heart as well as a change-maker, a tough secretary to a smuggler's widow, Johnny Toledo, the Donald Trump of the inner-city junk pile, and a kid who should have been hammering out engine blocks like his great-grandfather and playing in a garage band on weekends but was instead about to go to prison on a patch of volcanic ash that was only barely U.S. soil. A cross section of the community, when you thought about it, now that all the auto millions were draining into the eastern hemisphere. In one way or another I'd made all their troubles my own.

But that's my working method. Whenever I'm faced with a problem, I identify it, analyze it, and make it bigger.

There wasn't much to watch after the news now that my basic cable had been shut off for bills outstanding, just a lot of people yelling at one another without a script and a drama about a fifty-year-old woman and her three forty-year-old daughters. I turned in early.

The dream was the same, but I'd been through it so often I recognized it for what it was and did some light editing. Knowing the impact was coming front and rear, I slumped down in the driver's seat and let my muscles go limp. The crunch when it came was just as sickening, with the novelty of having become dreary from repetition. I might as well have stuck with the tube.

I sat up, groped among the day's refuse on the nightstand, and lit a cigarette, watching the smoke drift toward the source of light, in broken frames like an image in a silent film. For some reason it always seeks the light.

My head cleared a little more slowly. I realized the smoke was going in the wrong direction, away from the moon shining through the window and around the edge of the bedroom door standing half open. The lamp was on in the living room.

As I was trying to remember whether I'd turned it off, something clinked. It sounded like metal on glass.

I screwed out the cigarette in the ashtray on the night-stand—it seemed to make as much noise as someone dragging an iron safe through gravel—and reached inside the drawer I kept open with the .38 inside.

With my fingers closed around the cold grip I slid the covers to one side and tried to keep springs from scraping against each other as I swung bare feet to the floor. The nights were getting cooler. The touch of the boards made me feel naked in my shorts.

The something clinked again as I eased around the edge

of the door. Once clear, I paused to let my eyes catch up to the light. The lamp was on its lowest setting, a soft yellow glow in a room crowded with the unfamiliar shadows that gathered in a place I knew well every other hour of the day and night. Someone was sitting in my armchair. I couldn't tell if the figure was male or female.

It moved then. Something glittered, accompanied by that metallic sound. Then it settled back into motionless silence.

I kept close to the wall far from the light, but I wasn't fooling anyone. Two sharp clicks broke the stillness into three pieces and I blinked in the glare of the bulb at full power. My finger tightened on the trigger.

Mary Ann Thaler was looking at me with the same quiet tension she brought to bear on every situation. Her legs were crossed and an inch and a half of medium-dark liquid glistened in the bottom of one of my old-fashioneds. She lowered her other hand from the switch on the lamp, lifted the glass, and sipped, causing the ice cubes floating inside to shift and touch the side with a clink. My blood resumed circulating with a rush like warm water. I relaxed.

"There's nothing wrong with your lock," she said. "Just your door. The wood's shrunk away from the frame. I used an emery board on the latch."

"It's a wonder there aren't more woman burglars." I laid the revolver on the end table by the sofa.

I didn't feel any more self-conscious than usual. She'd seen me in my underwear under similarly unromantic circumstances. I watched her, fascinated. I'd never seen her drink anything stronger than white wine.

She swirled the stuff in the glass. "So this is what the fuss is about. They should stick to golf."

"My brand barely qualifies as Scotch. Are you going to finish it?"

"Be my guest." She set it down next to the lamp.

When I stepped forward to pick it up, she uncrossed her legs in transparent hose and crossed them the other way. Her years with the Detroit Police Department and now with Washington probably showed somewhere, but not in that light. She was slender and brown-haired, wearing it long now, and had on something tailored with an above-the-knee skirt that looked like tweed but moved like silk when she moved. Her shoes, narrow pumps with low heels for chasing terrorists, were on the floor beside the chair, one over on its side. I'd always admired her feet. I emptied the glass in one slow smooth motion and crunched the cubes.

She shuddered. "I hate a man who chews ice. If you ever wondered why we never hooked up, that's reason three hundred and ninety-nine."

"I thought I was the one playing hard to get." I got rid of the glass. "How are you, Marshal?"

"Deputy. I'm three suicide bombers shy of a promotion. I'm tired, if you really want to know. My section chief got me out of bed."

"Did he break in?"

"We reserve that for civilians. Get dressed. There were laws in this town last I heard."

"You haven't been listening very hard. Are we going anyplace special?"

"Not far. You know the way. We found this on the body."

I took the card she'd slipped from inside her blouse. It felt warm. I read my name on the front and my cell written on the back in my scrawl. "Could you narrow it down?"

SEVEN

We'll talk in the car," she said. "We may both be back in bed before the fighting roosters crow in Mexicantown."

There were several responses to that, but only one that would sustain what good relations we had. I put on loafers, slacks, a T-shirt, and came out shrugging into a Windbreaker to find her standing with her shoes on. I glanced at my revolver on the end table. She opened her coat to show me a Smith & Wesson Ladysmith on her slim suede belt, a semiautomatic designed for small hands and large exit wounds. I accompanied her unarmed.

She'd drawn a Chrysler with a government plate, black trim on a white finish, with an interior done in shades of gray.

"See the news last night?" She drove with her seat shoved all the way back and both arms extended straight to the wheel, like the pilot of a street chopper.

"Not since six o'clock. Did another mayor resign?"

"It's the same show three times a day. They should tape it at noon and send the personnel home."

"I saw the stuff on heroin O.D.s." I was cagy suddenly. I had an idea now where we were headed.

"That's city, and the boys in Narco are welcome to it, the arrogant pricks. One of our local entrepreneurs—in an honest racket—lost some merchandise in a break-in. If you left the room to pee you missed it."

"I leave the room more often than I used to. What made it worth sending a TV crew?"

"It had to do with high-definition electronics. They can tie that into advertising revenue. A neighborhood shopping sheet, that's what journalism's turned into. The entrepreneur used part of his face time to show off something the burglars missed on the first pass."

"The first pass?" I regretted chewing those ice cubes. They made a ball in my gut.

"They came back for it, we think. Anyway it isn't there."

"Who's we?"

"The DPD and the U.S. Department of Justice. Well, me. I got the account because of my long and cordial association with local authority."

"Long, anyway. Why the interest at Justice?"

"That's classified for now."

"You don't even sound like a cop anymore."

"Don't try to flatter me."

We cruised for a while in silence. The same ragged man was sitting on the same curb with all his chattel tied up in bags, distributed the same way as the morning before. He wasn't eating this time—hadn't, maybe, since he'd finished whatever he'd had in the greasy paper—just dangling his hands between his knees in jersey gloves with the fingers cut out, staring into the middle ground and waiting for the bus to a better place.

More intersections, and we were the only traffic crossing; we might have been in an automobile commercial. The Walgreen's where I'd run into Sergeant Mansanard rolled past, drenched in brilliant incandescence with the identical number of cars parked in a protective cluster in the vast lot. I had the feeling that if I went inside I'd find the big cop staked out on the same patch of linoleum, as if the last twenty-four hours hadn't happened. He, the store, and the homeless man on the curb might've been part of another recurring dream. Maybe I was dreaming now. Nothing is real at that hour of the morning.

Thaler was thinking along similarly cosmic lines. "I keep expecting something about this place to change, even for the worse. Any variety would do. There's a Taurus in a ditch off the Reuther that qualifies for historic status under the charter. Probably a whole family of Micronesians living there behind the citations on the windshield."

The conversation was turning in a safe, direction. I nudged it farther off the burner. "What made you put in for this job?"

"I wanted to see the world."

We turned onto Marcus, and that was the end of the small talk. "Someone called nine-one-one last night and hung up," she said. "Police responded, of course. Victim's name is Crossgrain, but you knew that."

"You can't make that case just because he had one of my cards. I stick them in magazines on drugstore racks."

"From the location and position of the body," she went on, "they thought at first he fell downstairs, but a lot more was broken about the place than just his bones. He put up a fight, but he was overmatched."

The brick house looked almost gaudy in the glare of police searchbeams and ribbons of yellow tape, satellite trucks quarantined in the nosebleed section thirty feet from the front walk.

"A lot of media we're having," I said. "I thought you had to be dismembered and eaten to make breaking news."

"They've got footage on this one, alive and well, only hours old. A thing like that drives up the stock." She stopped in the middle of the lane and killed the motor. That got the attention of neighbors with robes and overcoats thrown on over their pajamas and from the people standing fully dressed near the TV trucks. Thaler fixed me with her amber gaze. "Heel. Whatever you do, don't make eye contact."

We got out and hit the tsunami head on. Feet pattered, voices rose, strobes broiled unprotected skin. The deputy marshal didn't break stride. When a gap opened she plunged into it and I followed. She flashed brass at a uniform in crowd control, who held up the tape for us to duck under while others moved in to plug the leak. The noise behind us subsided into a collective groan: the voice of the Fourth Estate.

The cardboard was missing from the broken pane in the door. Crossgrain couldn't have made things easier if he'd left it wide open. All the ground-floor lights were burning, including a dusty ceiling fixture in the narrow bare entryway. It looked like we'd crashed an unsuccessful party.

The kitchen seemed somehow less cheerful with all the under-the-counter lights ablaze as well as the fluorescent overhead, but modern morgues are always bright. A detective I recognized from Homicide, a man with the long face and large hands of a yankee farmer, sat at the table where I'd drunk coffee, playing solitaire with Polaroids; he was stirring to rise when Thaler swung open the cellar door and I trailed her down the earth-smelling steps. At the bottom, someone had drawn a figure in abstract with masking tape, bending it up over the edge of the last step to suggest a stylized human foot in profile. I almost collided with Thaler from behind when she stopped to curse at it.

"I told that creep medical examiner not to move him till I got back."

A gob of animated flesh waddled into the base of the stairwell and planted a pair of square-toed oxfords on top of the tape. "*I* told him to take him back to the barn. This is my crime scene."

"Sergeant Hornet." The deputy marshal's tone flattened. You couldn't have pushed a spatula under it.

"Lieutenant. Remember? They kicked me upstairs when I transferred back from city hall. I got Alderdyce's old job."

"How could I have forgotten."

"You and me, Mary Ann, we're movin' on up to the East Side." He actually sang it. His high-pitched tenor was nasty enough when he spoke. "Not like Walker, there. He's been stuck in the same rut so long he thinks it's the penthouse."

You could talk yourself out of how fat Hornet was when you weren't actually in his presence; the imagination plays cartoonish pranks when you're standing close to the source, and the department has physical fitness standards. Then you ran into him again, almost always without expecting it, and you saw a massive coronary waiting for the paperwork. His green sportcoat hadn't buttoned since Molly Ringwald mattered and the waistline of his crumpled tan Dockers made a smiley face under one of those bellies you wanted to look away from but couldn't, like the aftermath of a high-school massacre. An amethyst the size of a duck's egg fastened a bolo tie on a shirt with an amphibian embroidered above the pocket. I decided he had excellent fashion sense. No one dresses that badly by accident.

Thaler said, "You're standing on evidence."

He looked down, but left his feet where they were. He took what she'd said on faith. There was no way he could see them. He made a noise like a teakettle with a stuck valve; he thought he was chuckling. "Oh, that. Memorize it for your grandkids. In a few years the photogs will snap the stiffs in three-D digital, prints too. The prosecution will project holograms for the jury. No more powder, no more tape, no more chalk. Best of all, no more dweebs from forensics getting Clearasil stains on everything. Virtual crime scene." He looked up. "*My* crime scene."

"We had this all worked out between the MacNamara Building and Thirteen Hundred. It's a cooperative effort."

"I worked it out with the department manual. This is city jurisdiction." He stuck a finger at me. "The only reason I let him get this far is he's a material witness."

I said, "And here I thought you liked to have me around to scratch behind the ears."

I was standing two steps behind and above Thaler, close enough to iron my shirt in the steam from her ears. It cooled by half degrees. When she spoke it sounded like conversation.

"We'll sort things out during business hours, after I talk to my chief. I don't suppose you'd object to *sharing* the investigation until then?"

"When you put it that way, I'd be an asshole to refuse."

"The suspense is killing me," I said. "Is it yes or no?"

His face, which under ordinary circumstances was the gay shade of chopped sirloin, darkened. *This is it,* his aorta seemed to be saying, and I was sorry for the sake of the city budget he'd sent away the morgue wagon. Then he backed up, turned, and paddled deeper into the basement and out of sight.

Thaler spoke low over her shoulder. "Try to tie a knot in it for an hour. This country's in no shape for another civil war."

EIGHT

We'd missed the crowd. A prowl-car officer in uniform was tamping down a yawn in an uncluttered corner and one of Hornet's forensics dweebs, a slender youth with a Brazilian-wax goatee, was shutting up his evidence case, showing no sign of having heard the lieutenant's remark. A chemical smell of acetate sharpened the air and patches of fingerpint powder—white on dark surfaces, black on lights—decorated everything an intruder might have touched. Crossgrain had gotten his thorough job in the end.

The basement didn't bear much resemblance to the tidy browser-friendly place I'd visited twenty hours earlier. The ends of the aisles of merchandise nearest the stairs looked as if they'd collapsed under their own weight: Sleek, early atomage small kitchen appliances lay in heaps; a set of steel utility shelves had been dumped over, spilling its cargo of portable radios, Roy Rogers board games, whimsical cookie jars, and bolts of upholstery fabric onto the concrete floor; someone had put a foot or an elbow or his head through the picture tube of an Admiral TV in a walnut cabinet.

Blood made a zigzag trail on the floor from the debris to the taped outline at the base of the stairs. The round spots were so nearly perfect I'd have thought they'd been stenciled there if I hadn't known they weren't there before.

Mary Ann Thaler pointed at the trail. "He made a break for it while they were knocking him around, got to the stairs and maybe three steps up before he was tackled, hit his head on the floor or got hit with something as hard, and that's the story on Reuben Crossgrain. Is that how you make it, Lieutenant?"

The red splotch inside the tape didn't look stenciled.

"That or he tripped on his feet and fell. M.E. said most of his ribs were busted on top of the skull fracture, his right eye socket—orbit, he calls it—nose, jaw. Jaw almost torn clean off. Honey of a working over, and not beginner's luck."

"How many?" I asked.

Thaler said, "Two or more." Hornet said, "One." It was simultaneous. They looked at each other. "Beating like that," Thaler said, "someone had to hold him while the other got busy."

Hornet shook his head; parts of it kept moving after he stopped. "No pressure marks or ligatures on the arms, M.E. said. Somebody stood him up like a heavy bag and went to town."

"Baseball bat?" I said.

That was a minor mistake, but they both picked up on it. Hornet spoke first. "How'd you know there was a baseball bat?"

"It's what I'd use if I ever wanted to play the violin again. Beating a grown man bare-handed is rough on both ends."

"He had your card in his shirt pocket."

I laughed. He reddened.

"An aluminum bat turned up in the upstairs bedroom," Thaler said before he could erupt, "next to a smashed lamp from the nightstand. He was getting ready to turn in; all he had on was a corny bowling shirt and boxers, pair of socks. His pants were folded over the back of a chair. He hears a noise, picks up the bat, but he doesn't make it out of the room. The bat gets taken away from him and tossed, smashing the lamp. Then he gets frog-marched downstairs to show where he kept the TV converter box he had on the news."

Hornet said, "We don't know that's all he came for."

"It hasn't shown up, even in this mess. Crossgrain had eighty-nine dollars in his wallet upstairs, a wristwatch, all untouched. Everything's orderly up there except for the lamp. Without an inventory of the stock it's unlikely we'll ever know what else might have been taken."

"Speak for yourself, Marshal Dillon," said the lieutenant. "The department didn't get dumber after you left."

She bore in tight, sparing him the obvious but clever rejoinder. "The box is important, that much we know. It got overlooked the first time and someone came back for it after he saw Crossgrain with it on TV. I don't buy random burglaries at the same house two nights in a row, even in this town. Also he wasn't beaten up for kicks. He was never intended to leave this basement alive."

I asked how she knew that. Dark patches showed on her cheeks, as if she'd outrun her better instincts, but they faded quickly. She looked at the kid from the lab. I'd almost forgotten he was there. "Tell him."

Hornet said, "We're withholding that from the public."

"Walker isn't public. He's barely a citizen. I didn't bring

him here just as a witness. He's sat in on more homicide investigations than Boston Blackie."

"Who the hell's that?"

I was a little vague on it myself, but she made an impatient noise and told the kid again to tell me. But he was afraid of the fat lieutenant and hesitated. Thaler said, "He wasn't beaten with a bat or a lead pipe or a Hummer or the National Bank of Detroit. The killer used his hands and feet, nothing else. You don't waste a man with talent like that on your garden-variety B and E."

"You're the medical examiner?" I asked the kid. He didn't look like a creep, just shoved out into the world with the crust still soft.

He flicked a glance at Hornet, then shook his head and cleared his throat. I expected his voice to crack, but he'd been through all that. "I'm blood and semen."

"He's the M.E.'s pet," Thaler said. "He's first-year med at the U of M. The doc opened Crossgrain's shirt and asked him if he saw anything significant about the bruises on the chest and abdomen."

"Chiefly the costal cartilages." Enthusiasm overcame fear. The kid couldn't stand by and let a layman botch the story. "If you're going to use *abdomen,* you could at least say thorax too and be consistent. Subcutaneous hemorrhage patterns not in conformity with blows from a single blunt instrument," he said. "Clear contact evidence of phalanges, metacarpals, metatar—"

"Hands and feet," translated the deputy marshal. "One of the kung fu boys."

I had a sudden image of Gale Kreski in his music store, going into fighting stance. I erased it. Even a lunk like Hornet had been a cop long enough to learn to read minds.

But I wasn't fast enough for Thaler, who caught the expression on my face if not what made it.

"You were here. Walker. Not because one of your cards turned up, and not just because we say it. You were here because Sergeant Ivan Mansanard, a fifteen-year veteran with the Tactical Mobile Division, caught the squeal on the first burglary at this address and put you on to Crossgrain as a personal favor. It's up to Lieutenant Hornet whether Mansanard faces a disciplinary hearing for sharing police information with a civilian before he filed his report with his superiors. Did you think Homicide wouldn't talk to the responding officer when that complaint scrolled up on the computer?"

"No kidding, his first name's Ivan?"

Hornet wobbled his chins at the uniformed officer in his corner. "Read this character his rights. Obstruction of justice for starters. Leave plenty of room at the bottom of the report."

The cop abandoned the yawn he'd been building and came out of his slouch, unhooking the cuffs from his belt; a quiet couple of hours until the end of his tour, gone up in smoke.

I said, "Hadn't you better ask me if I was here, so I can lie about it first? You can't make a case for obstruction until then."

Hornet gestured, halting the uniform. He glared at Thaler. "What'd he tell you on the way over?"

"I'm a woman; I did most of the talking. He's right, I didn't ask. Acting coy when I brought up the card isn't even a misdemeanor yet."

"Your people will get around to it," I said. "You've been busy tapping wires and waterboarding suspects. I don't know how you get done as much as you do."

Hornet fluttered his lips in an accurate approximation of a fart. He was an eloquent man when all was said and done.

I went on. "All you had to do was pick up a phone. Instead, you broke into my house, drank my liquor, told me to get dressed and come along for a ride. I didn't ask where; I pay my taxes, it's in your best interest to keep me healthy and solvent. Healthy anyway. At the end of the ride is a fat circus wagon I don't enjoy being in the same room with even in the daytime, who offers to hang chains on me because I laughed at him. With angels like you looking out for me, who the hell needs devils?"

Thaler said, "Is that really a thing? I've seen you fake tantrums before."

I moved a shoulder. "The Hornet part. The rest was okay seeing as how it was you."

"You're no picnic yourself, pal." The lieutenant was redder than ever. I wondered if there was a pool downtown on just when he'd throw a piston rod and if I could get in. But I had an unfair advantage. Some people walk around with all their buttons exposed.

"Were you here?" Thaler asked.

I smiled. "Now, was that so hard?"

"Cuff him," Hornet said. "I'll take the reprimand."

The officer hovered, jingling his manacles back and forth like a slinky. He wasn't a collector of bad paper like his lieutenant.

"That's one sure way of shutting him up for good," Thaler said.

"Now say something that sounds bad."

She made no response, kept her eyes on me.

I nodded finally. "I was here yesterday morning. I made my pitch and Crossgrain bought it; three days' worth, anyway, to hunt down his property. He got one."

She asked me what I'd found out.

"Just that the first day on a case is a waste of daylight, but I already knew that. That's why I didn't put the bottle away."

"Who'd you talk to?" she asked.

"I blew my time. Blowing yours too would be extravagant."

"I'll be the judge of that. Your client's dead. Why tease?"

"If he weren't, you wouldn't have gotten that much. That's the private part of 'private investigator.' I can't compete against the public sector without it."

"That's not much encouragement to keep a leash on Hornet."

"If I *was* on a leash, it sure as hell wouldn't be you holding it," he said.

"I heard you before, Lieutenant; it's your crime scene. Until it isn't." She reached up to adjust the glasses she hadn't worn since the operation. She frowned when she realized her mistake. "What's your theory on what went down here. Walker? Even a busted slot pays off if you whack it often enough."

"In that case I'm overdue for a jackpot." I looked at the vintage TVs, saw only my funhouse reflection in the bulging glass. "They were after the box all right. Crossgrain showed it to me so I'd know what to look for. It was a sample he ordered before committing himself to an entire shipment. That's why it wasn't with the others. When he flashed it on television, they came back for it—him, too. He wasn't home the first time, or we wouldn't be having this conversation. Your investigation would be at least twenty-four hours older and those cottonmouths outside would be the only reason I knew about it at all."

"Kind of an alternate universe," she said. "What makes you so sure they'd have killed him then?"

"You said yourself it was a hit, planned and executed. When wouldn't matter."

"We know the when. We need the why."

"Homicide needs the why," I said. "It usually leads to the who. That's their end game, but for you it's just the jumping-off place. That's why you're here, snarling at Hornet over the same gnawed-over bone."

We locked glances for a little. She was as hard to read as always. She turned to Hornet. "A favor. Sergeant."

"Lieutenant."

"Sorry. For some reason you'll always be sergeant to me."

"Yeah, I got the common touch. What?"

"Send your people home."

"You got something against overtime?"

"You're in charge, as you keep reminding me, so what I have to say includes you, but that's as far as my clearance goes."

"What about Walker?"

"You've had almost as much experience with him as I have. How many people do you know who served jail time more than once for not opening up? I'm talking people, not career crooks. The first time usually cures them. I don't think he's publishing his memoirs anytime soon."

"Who'd buy them?" I asked.

He let that steep, then told the uniform and the apprentice medical examiner to take it on the ankles. "If Siddons is still in the kitchen, tell him to wait in the car. He can play with the radio."

The cop found his feet and the kid hoisted his case. After the door closed at the top of the stairs we waited for the front door to do the same. When it had, Thaler looked around.

"They—he—whatever—didn't make this mess looking for that box," she said. "The energy was better spent messing up our vic until he told them where they could find what they wanted. That gave them a head start on the rest of what they came for."

I found a cigarette in a pocket of my Windbreaker and played with it, just to have something to occupy my hands. The smell from the chemical they'd used to test for blood or whatever impressed me as too volatile for striking matches. In any case my bad leg was aching more than my lungs. "He dialed nine-one-one, you said?"

Hornet answered for her. "Someone did. Caller ID put a lot of trace experts out of work, but it's sure faster."

"He showed me a doohickey that lets him surf through menus using an old-fashioned rotary phone."

"So that's what that was," he said. "He had it in his pocket with your card."

Crossgrain hadn't changed clothes. Many people who worked at home didn't bother often. I seemed to remember he'd smelled a little musty, like old magazines stored in a damp corner. Plenty of people I'd had to deal with smelled worse. Hornet's aftershave would kill a gnat at ten paces.

I said, "That's what bothers me. It's a wonder Master Po waited while he dialed."

Thaler and Hornet exchanged looks. "We figured he had a cell with his home number on it and called the emergency line as he was breaking for the stairs," the lieutenant said. "We didn't find one, but we assumed the killer took it with him for some reason."

"I wasn't told that." Butter wouldn't melt in Thaler's mouth. Iron might.

"And you're so good at sitting on information we agreed to withhold."

I broke up the fight. "Crossgrain preferred old for old's sake, just like his customer base. He wouldn't have had a cell. Your killer called nine-one-one from the landline and hung up on his way out. He wanted the victim found as early as possible."

"Some kind of warning," said Thaler. "Shape up or else."

"Your turn. Deputy." I smoothed the cigarette between two fingers and put it back in the pack.

PART TWO

WEAR AND TERROR

NINE

We never had this conversation," Thaler said.

"We haven't had it yet." It was impossible to tell when Hornet was being thick on purpose.

"Let's just have it," I said. "It'll be on the Drudge Report tomorrow whatever we do."

"Let's pretend it won't and practice shutting up." She looked from him to me. I tried looking earnest back. "The terrorists are running out of money."

I said, "I knew it was going to be terrorists. I'm stopping on the way home and buying a lottery ticket."

Hornet told me to shut the fuck up. "I knew they were running low on suicide bombers. I didn't know they were strapped for cash. We taking up a collection?"

"Now you shut the fuck up," she said. "We suspected a suicide bomber crunch when they went to women, who as we know are five-cent returnables in the Islamic world; no forty virgins and a trip to Miami Beach for them. We were sure of it when they went to mental defectives."

"As opposed to fanatics who are mentally sound." Every

Leap Year, Hornet makes an intelligent remark. It was almost worth waiting for.

Thaler let it coast. "Attrition loses most wars. The side less capable of replacing personnel and equipment sues for peace. That's a matter of economics, not dedication. God knows these sand barons can chuck a rock in any direction in their hemisphere and hit a pocket of reinforcements. But those recruits have to be fed and supplied with arms and transportation and methods of communicating with each other and their command. You can't just stroll into the Baghdad Walmart and load up on TracFones on credit."

Hornet said, "I've got to dip into equity to fill up at a Mobil station. I thought most of that money went straight into Sheikh Asscrack's mattress."

"But it isn't coming back out. The oil emirs like to see our buildings fall down, but when push comes to shove they like their gold-plated belly dancers and Atlantic-size swimming pools more, especially when the return on their investment isn't as spectacular as it was in the beginning. They're spoiled by fast profits and expect the same from their intrigues. Well, the Blessed Struggle is bogged down worse than we are over there, and the hose has sprung plenty of leaks.

"At the top of the food chain, the money's moved the same way as on Wall Street, through offshore accounts by electronic transfer, but a bushel of zeroes on a computer printout won't buy a handful of grain or a box of shells in the Syrian Desert. Before entering the theater of war the securities are converted into hard cash and shipped by truck and pack animal and on Omar's back. The temptation's too much for anyone but a foam-at-the-mouth lunatic, and those are nowhere near as common as they look in those government-staged protests on CNN. Everyone takes his cut, from General Buck Abdullah on down to Private First Class Billy Joe Mohammed. The amount that makes it to the weapons bazaars scores barely enough dynamite to blow the head off a Barbie doll."

"Greed." Hornet was grinning. "I knew we'd come up with an export they can use."

"We and our Arab allies can claim partial credit for the shortfall when we froze the assets of known terrorist supporters in the U.S. and the Middle East. The purse strings are tight."

I said, "I'm enjoying this as much as Hornet, especially the clever names for Islamic fascists, but we were discussing how to get *Girls Gone Wild* on your Motorola after HDTV kicks in." Actually I saw a glimmer of light, but I wanted to catch her before the slide projector came out.

"When Congress passed that law requiring all commercial stations to switch to digital, they created the biggest cash cow this country has seen since the tobacco settlement. That's where we think the terrorists are raising funds now. Ever hear of MacArthur Industries?"

My eyes strayed to the spot where Crossgrain had put the sample converter box in my hands; but we were all out in the open now. "That's the outfit our stiff ordered from," I said. "No one else in town seems to have heard of it." I deliberately blocked out Eugenia Pappas' little hesitation when I'd mentioned the name. I couldn't pack up the poker face just yet.

"*I'd* heard of it. I read the briefings from Washington. So far, though, you and Crossgrain and the news crew that interviewed him yesterday were the only ones to have actually *seen* one of the converters. We haven't been able to identify a single customer. One of our people happened to be watching when the camera moved in on the manufacturer's plate." She heard herself and frowned. "Okay, he happened to be watching because he happens to be employed to monitor all the local media. It's a couch potato's dream job and he takes it seriously."

"So that's why I got feds in my pants," said Hornet. "Took you long enough to clue me in."

"It took almost that long to get the information through channels. The first police team was on the scene when I came to talk to Crossgrain."

"Thank Christ. I was starting to think you had a mole in the CID."

"If we did, I wouldn't be told. I don't have that kind of clearance."

"Shit. I bet it's Siddons. He couldn't find wax in his ear."

I said, "MacArthur has a drop box in Southfield. I don't guess that's news."

"It's got boxes in fourteen cities across the continent, including Toronto, where we think they're shipping the merchandise into North America, only not through that box. The Canadians think nine-eleven was a capital jest, but so far no one's crashed a plane into—I don't know; a statue of Benedict Arnold?" She had a grudge of some sort against our neighbors across the river. I think her uncle was killed by a moose. "Where you order from determines which plate they screw on the back. We think. It's the biggest shell game in the world.

"The reason we're looking so hard at MacArthur is it's the only company trading in the converters we haven't been able to trace directly to its headquarters. The snarl of dummy addresses, holding companies, subsidiaries, sub-subsidiaries, and sub-*sub*-subsidiaries makes the search for the Nile look like a ride through the Tunnel of Love."

"Crossgrain told me he ordered from an eight hundred number," I said. "You must've been able to trace that."

"It led to a boiler room where the operators process the incoming through an Internet address. When we tried tracking it, we got so much spam it shut the District down for four hours."

Hornet and I stood silent while she collected her thoughts, appreciating her ordeal. The lieutenant belched.

She went on. "Some of the companies we connected with MacArthur are legitimate corporations trading on the New York Stock Exchange and in Tokyo. Their CEOs say they never heard of MacArthur, and we're not so sure they're all lying. It's the supernumeraries who look after the nuts and bolts; nailing the right clerk or secretary or junior exec is like trying to tail one bee in a swarm. We don't have the people, and when I say *we* I'm including the FBI and the CIA and Homeland Security and the intelligence divisions of all the branches of the U.S. military."

"Wow," Hornet said, when she ran down finally. "It almost makes me sorry I don't give a rat's ass."

She let him have her cool brown gaze. "Maybe you will when someone drives a car bomb through Thirteen Hundred."

"It already looks like someone did. You been away a while, so you forgot what police do. Walker's right, for once: When somebody's careless enough to drop a corpse in our streets like a turd, it's our job to scrape it up. If we can find out who dropped it, we flush it and go home, just like a guy walking his dog with a plastic bag.

"I ain't spy material. For one thing I'm too fat to jump on

roofs and hook up with shady characters in rug shops, and for another I don't have that kind of time. I just had a file dumped on my desk that went cold two years ago. It's still cold. No new evidence, no witnesses we didn't talk to ten, twelve times, just a family member that hit it off with the attorney general over a plate of spaghetti in Lansing last month, but it's open again and that's that, we make room for it next to all these heroin overdoses and now Crossgrain. If you can tell me why he had to die just because he took delivery on a shipment of legal merchandise, then I'll give a rat's ass." He waited, watching her with his mean little pig eyes folded in suet.

It was a barn-burner from start to finish. I wouldn't have thought he had the wind to get through it.

"I can't tell you until I have a chance to examine the merchandise," she said. "So far, Walker's the only person with a pulse who's gotten close enough to touch it." She looked at me, expectation dripping all over.

"I hefted it is all. I've held heavier Manhattans."

To Hornet she said, "I don't give a rat's ass why Crossgrain was killed if finding out doesn't lead me to who sent the shipment."

"I'm just after the shipment," I said. "If anyone's asking."

"You're a lame duck," said Thaler. "Your client's in the shop with a cracked block."

"Where I can't give him a refund. I still owe two days on the retainer."

"It won't do his ghost any good if you spend 'em sitting in a cell at County," Hornet said.

"I'm confused. Am I a lame duck or a rat's ass?"

The deputy marshal moved in close to Hornet and said

something in a low voice. He pushed out his paunch and flattened his hands against his kidneys, like a pregnant woman with a bad back, and turned away from me, burying his response in two and a half feet of blubber and polyester. I felt like a customer in a butcher shop getting ready to buy two pounds of thumb.

When they were facing me again Thaler said, "How about staked goat?"

I asked what it paid.

"Two days on the street," Hornet said, "no interference from us. All you got to do to thank us is come running back with whatever you get."

"If it's all the same to you I'll take the jail time. I can use the R and R."

He said, "That's a bluff we can call. Me and the marshal."

"Deputy," she said.

"International terrorism amps up the volume. The city can't house you without a charge, but Deputy Marshal Thaler can dock you in the Milan Federal Correctional Institution for reasons of national security, same old specialty of the house. The Bill of Rights don't exist when the republic's at stake."

"Why not Guantanamo? I can top up my tan."

"There's a three-month waiting list for admission to Gitmo," Thaler said. "Can't think why. The food's better in Milan. Justice likes to keep its prisoners fat and sluggish."

I stuck a hand in my pocket and turned the cigarette pack over and over. "Who would I report to?"

"Me." Once again they spoke at the same time.

Another brief conference with Hornet's back turned my way. You could have projected *Lawrence of Arabia* on it.

Thaler moved out of his shadow. "Me, if you get a line on

those converters. The lieutenant if you turn a suspect. Copy us both, of course."

Hornet said, "If you lose our numbers, I'll book you on obstruction and interfering with the police in the performance of their duties."

"Same old specialty of the house," I said.

"Except by then we'll have everything we need to shake loose a warrant. That's the part that sold me: If you don't follow through, the deal never happened. Can't recommend the diet at County," he said. "Beanie-wienies and sauerkraut from the can."

"Two days without fuzz steaming up my collar," I said. "That's like two weeks in real time."

Mary Ann Thaler took me home and I chased sleep for an hour. When it finished outrunning me I got up and made coffee. An unfamiliar car was parked on the street a few doors down. Someone with foresight had driven it through a mud puddle, but it was the latest model for three blocks. I didn't know if it belonged to Detroit or Washington, but either way it violated the terms of our deal. I drank from my cup and watched it though the window with mixed emotions. I'd traded a counterfeit bill for a blind horse. It was an honorable arrangement that no one intended to honor.

TEN

I sat down in the living room with my coffee and dialed a number I knew by heart. On the other end, the bell was hooked up to an air horn to be heard above the whine of power wrenches.

"*Ja.*" Ernst Dierdorf picked up just ahead of AT&T.

"A little heavy on the Teutonic this morning."

"Oh. It's you." He racheted back the accent. He had a thousand customers and knew each one by voice. His ears were tuned to tell which belt was loose by its whistle and whether a rattle belonged to a stuck lifter or a broken engine mount.

I said I needed a loaner.

"You bang up that Cutlass again?"

"That was just once, and years ago. It's fine. Just too easy to spot."

I told him what I needed. The arrangements were involved, but he listened without interrupting and didn't ask me to repeat anything. He said to sit tight and broke the connection.

OK Towing & Repair was an outlaw garage, operating in open violation of federal law. Neither he nor any of his employees was a certified mechanic, and no framed proof of certification hung on any of his walls. Overnight, the legislation, which was intended to discourage incompetence and price-gouging, had destroyed the old American custom of a garage on every corner and quadrupled the cost of even the most basic repairs. Ernst, who had left Germany with his father to avoid just that kind of tampering with private enterprise, kept a mean little rat terrier of an attorney on a leash to stay in business.

When I finished the pot and put on another, the unfamiliar car was still in the same place, all alone now that my neighbors had all left for work. I couldn't tell if anyone was inside. There would be two: one to drive, the other to get out and tail me on foot in case I took the last parking space.

A knuckle banged on the back door. I let Ernst in while the coffee was brewing and shook his hand. "I expected you to send a flunky."

"I have a vested interest in that car. I raised it from a wing nut. You're lucky I let *you* drive it."

It was the first time I'd seen him without coveralls. He wore a plaid sport coat over a blue denim shirt, narrow necktie, and jeans. Nothing fit him properly; his hunched, shriveled frame would challenge a master tailor. A jack or something had slipped early in his working life, crushing parts of him that had been replaced with titanium and plastic. The thought of him dragging himself over fences to get to my house unobserved made me cringe.

I let him peer around the edge of the curtain at the unfamiliar car outside. He made a disgusted noise with his tongue against his teeth. "Designed in Canada, assembled in Mexico with parts made in China. Like feeding yourself with a fork, a corn tortilla, and chopsticks."

"Coffee?"

"Strong?"

"Brutal."

He took plenty of sugar. I was pretty sure he was on his third set of teeth. His head with its thickness of blonde hair—graying now—and aging but clean lines needed a Heidelburg dueling scar on one cheek to complete the effect, but apart from his looks he was thoroughly Americanized. The accent only came out when he didn't want to disappoint a customer who preferred the stereotype.

"Sixty-five-and-a-half Skylark Gran Sport." He pushed a plain ring with two keys on it across the table in the breakfast nook. "White with patches of rust-red primer. It was scheduled for painting Friday. Four-oh-one Wildcat engine."

"I thought the Wildcat was four-forty-five."

"That's the number of pounds of torque it delivers at twenty-eight hundred RPM. Four-oh-one refers to cubic inches."

"I'm used to four-fifty-five in the Cutlass."

"You won't notice much difference. Buick called it 'a Howitzer with windshield wipers' in its advertising."

"Suspension?"

"Four control-arm in back, roll bar in front for stability. Boxed frame. Those were standard. I made some improvements." He looked smug.

I gave him the keys to the Cutlass.

"How fancy do you want it?" he asked. "I can keep 'em busy for twenty minutes, then I've got a brake job that can't wait."

"Ten should do it. Stick to the limit and don't let 'em get a good look at who's behind the wheel."

He finished his coffee. "I parked two streets over like you said, straight shot from your back door."

"Thanks, Ernst. What's the damage?"

"Don't scare me with such talk. Top off the tank—you've got additive?"

"I've got a case in the garage." Classic muscle cars won't run on modern unleaded gas without help.

"I put some in the trunk just in case. Fill it up when you're finished and get it back to me in one piece. I've got a customer on the hook with homes in Grosse Pointe and London. He wants to ship it back and forth across the Atlantic by air."

"The economy must not be so bad after all."

"Oh, he's hurting. He couldn't swing the asking on the forty-nine Merc he had his eyes on originally. You take the cure?"

I caught his meaning after a second. "Nope. Still smoking."

"Not in the car. I reupholstered it in red leather."

"At least let me pay your hourly rate."

"That's work. This cloak-and-dagger business beats the grease pit." An idea took some of the chill out of blue eyes. "What you can do, as long as you're not using the Cutlass, is let me bang out the dings and give it a spray job. I'll do it for cost. It's a sin to hide that engine inside a brown paper bag."

"I need the protective coloration. They'll shoot me if they think they can't catch me."

We stood and shook hands again. I reminded him to obey the traffic laws. Although he could dismantle a '55 Thunderbird convertible and reassemble it as a station wagon, he was an unreliable driver. They say Stradivari couldn't play a note.

As the garage door trundled shut, I watched the unfamiliar vehicle separate itself from the curb and fall in a block and a half behind my car. The distance made it a closed tail; I wasn't supposed to know it existed. This team must have been using a coloring book for a manual. If it was Washington, I hoped that meant they were saving their best people for actual terrorists. If it was Detroit, it was business as usual.

I was feeling athletic; my morning pills had kicked in. I let myself out the back door, hopped a fence and a drainage ditch, and found the Buick where Ernst had said I would, a two-door hardtop built wide and low to the ground. I'd been afraid it would attract too much attention, but the chalky white paint worn down to dull reddish-brown primer in big swatches on the hood and fenders blended in with most of the beaters on the street. A connoisseur would spot it for what it was, but I didn't plan to be driving it long enough to build an entourage.

The instruments in the dash were pleasantly simple, just a speedometer, odometer, and fuel and oil gauges and an AM radio, like in the Cutlass. Whoever had ordered it from the factory hadn't popped for air-conditioning or a tachometer, but Ernst had installed seat belts, also optional under LBJ. The interior smelled of good leather and the bucket seat embraced my back and hips with warmth from the sun.

It started with a discreet rumble, insulated by glass packs in the twin pipes. The transmission shifted smoothly and there was little play in the wheel. Just in case Hornet or Thaler was double-teaming me, I drove around the block, but no one who was behind me when I pulled out was still there when I finished.

I called Gale Kreski on the cell. He put me on hold to deal with a music-store customer, then came back on. A beat pulsed in the background: the same basic broth every rapper in two continents used for stock. That answered a question I hadn't intended to ask him, whether anyone in creation listened to hip-hop when he was alone.

I said, "There's been a development."

"Yeah, I watch the news. That your client in the morgue?"

"He paid up front. My offer's still good." I'd thought his generation got its current events from late-night comedy. "Just a couple of follow-up questions."

"I heard he was beaten to death. I didn't do it."

"That answers one." I wanted to ask him about Mac-Arthur Industries. I'd been distracted the first time by his tale of personal woe, but I wasn't about to do it over the telephone. I wanted to see him to find out if he'd react to the name the way Eugenia Pappas had seemed to.

"Listen, I got an appointment with my lawyer in thirty minutes. Try me this afternoon." *Just try*, his tone seemed to say. I said I would and hit END.

Ouida, the personal assistant, answered at the Pappas number. She sounded a little more friendly this morning, but in an impersonal professional way. She said her employer was out tending to charitable business.

"That's okay. It's you I wanted to talk to."

"I wouldn't waste your time, Mr. Walker. I'm still waiting to hear back from the people Mrs. Pappas asked me to make contact with. I'll call once I have—after I report to her." She hung up in my face, but not without saying good-bye, in an impersonal professional way.

I punched in another number and got the pawnbroker

who'd put me on to Pappas, Bud Lite, and Johnny Toledo. Him I asked point-blank about MacArthur. There was no getting a significant reaction from him, in person or over the air.

He at least didn't seem to have seen the news. "I admire your faith in the inflation rate," he said. "That money was for services rendered, not a deposit on the future."

"I'm headed away from your shop. Give me something worth turning around for at today's gas prices and I'll shower you with euros."

"The name don't ring a bell, but drop in sometime after I get a chance to poke around. I'm getting a little sick of buying back the same toaster oven from Mr. Willis."

I put away the cell. I don't know how I'd ever gotten along without it.

Sometimes the second day of an investigation is just a carbon copy of the first. You go back and plow the same tired ground hoping for a quarter acre of something more promising than dust.

Meanwhile I had some fun for as long as I had the loaner. Pulling away from a stop sign at the beginning of a long deserted block, I laid parallel black stripes on the asphalt and topped sixty before I had to slow for a changing light at the next intersection. The noise was a kind of mating call. As I sat waiting, feeling the idle vibrating in my crotch, a couple of kids with too much metal in their faces to have come from anywhere but the scrubbed-white suburbs slid alongside me in the outside lane.

They were driving a Plymouth Roadrunner rusted through at the wheel wells, as holey as Venetian lace. That meant they'd invested more of their parents' money in the plant than in the body. Recognizing the Gran Sport for a fellow dark horse, the kid in the passenger's seat hung a billy-goat beard out his window with a grin in it. I bared my teeth back. His buddy behind the wheel gunned twice and tore off at the green with a fine shriek of rubber he wasn't paying for, adding black smoke to his pre-existing carbon footprint. I gave him half a block for confidence, then blasted past his little 383.

I shot past a city cruiser tucked nose out inside a cracked half driveway ending in a tangle of weeds belonging to one of the fabled local empty lots. I throttled down, but the lights and siren came on. Just then the Roadrunner, accelerating to catch up, skinned within a sixty-fourth of an inch of the cruiser's left front fender. The officer in the driver's seat forgot about me and went after the bird in hand. As the kids turned obediently into the curb I gave them the Red Baron salute and spun around the corner. Okay, I'm a kid too. The piercing's optional.

Slowing to the limit, I slid the AM needle all the way left and right looking for something appropriate from Jan & Dean. I got a string of conservative yellfests and switched off. The '60s just aren't coming back.

Rain splatted the windshield out of a clear blue sky. The drops turned elliptical, then broke left and right in crooked patterns propelled by the slipstream. The sun stayed out. "The devil's whipping his wife," my grandmother used to say of that state of affairs; the drops were her tears. They're a prediction of doom of some kind. Nearly everything is, when you study the science of soothsaying. The tea leaves, sheep's entrails, and cast bones turn up positive omens about as often as valuable rookie cards.

———

The gaunt HUD house stood resolvedly in its garden of orange barbed wire and purple loosestrife, flora's attractive answer to the zebra mussel. The galvanized aluminum inner sleeve the city had installed to discourage squatters had been peeled back sardine-can fashion from the windows to let in air and light. Nothing appeared to have changed there since yesterday, or for that matter since the Pet Rock. The city continued its slug's crawl toward bleak oblivion around all four sides.

The rain, such as it was, had stopped short of wetting the earth. A rat the size of a young coyote was foraging inside a Dunkin' Donuts box in a burned-out patch in the grass. The rattling went on without pause as I climbed out of the driver's seat and thunked the door shut. It might have been a coyote at that; at night they gather in the basement of the demolished downtown Hudson's Department Store to howl at streetlights. Civilization isn't in nature's weight class when skunk cabbage grows wild in the neighborhoods.

I stood outside the ramshackle entrance Johnny Toledo had cut in the side of the house and called his name; called it twice. No one answered. He never left home. To do so in a wheelchair invited every bipedal predator from the primordial urban ooze to fall on him and strip him to his colostomy sack. I checked the load in the Chief's Special that had grafted itself to my skin, settled it gently into its clip for quick release, and heaved aside the jagged piece of siding that covered the hole, stepping back to fist the revolver. His boys' size .22 rifle carried a small round, but a greasy one that encouraged infection, gangrene, and a slow odoriferous death. I'd read *The Snows of Kilimanjaro*.

Nothing stirred except the rat grazing on crumbs and wind slithering through weeds.

The voice of experience told me not to go in. Not into a building that should have been torn down during another corrupt administration. The voice of experience should be a *basso profundo,* like Tennessee Ernie Ford's. Instead it's a mealy little whisper, like the teller's at a window informing you your acount's overdrawn.

In any case I was too old to wait for an administration that wasn't corrupt. I went in.

ELEVEN

At a glance, the place hadn't changed much in a day. There were more catalytic converters; the *Free Press* had reported a rash of thefts from cars and trucks parked on the northwest side overnight, probably for the platinum they contained. Like the other scrap they had their own pile. It was an orderly system despite appearances. An overturned wheelchair meant nothing because he had several in various stages of disassembly. You had to be a special kind of paraplegic to traffic in stolen wheelchairs; but Johnny never asked for any more sympathy than he gave. Business is business is business.

Then I saw something that reminded me I had a gun.

I tightened my grip on the butt and reached down with the other hand to lift a golden statuette off the floor where it had fallen when the folding TV tray had collapsed from under it. A fresh dent on the side of its head had turned the cherub into a mongoloid. It seemed a hell of a way to treat the only memento Johnny Toledo had of his father's adventures in the scrap trade.

As I was lowering it back to the floor, trying not to make any more noise than I already had, a floorboard shifted upstairs.

It wasn't Johnny. The house's second story had ceased to exist for him when he'd lost the use of his legs. As far as I could tell he slept in his wheelchair.

Sneaking up those stairs was impossible. If they'd ever had a padded runner, scavengers had made off with it before the Supremes broke up, and decades of unheated winters and humid summers had split and warped the boards into driftwood shapes; I'd have made less noise scampering across a piano keyboard. I took a deep breath and ran up them, feet and heart pounding, the gun heavy in my hand, hoping I wouldn't put a foot through and shoot myself in the head.

I stopped before my head came level with the landing. That easy I wasn't going to make it for anyone waiting up there with a gun. I waited, counting my heartbeats. He'd have to go through me to get out.

Wrong again. With a melancholy crash, the last glass pane in the house gave way.

I took the rest of the steps at a dead run and got to the open door of the first room off the stairs just in time to see a head of brown curls vanish through the window.

Three strides took me across the bare floor. At the window I flattened my back against the wall and edged an eye past the frame. No one shot at me. A small figure in a red jersey jacket with his shirttail flapping below the hem made a broken-field dash around the debris in the adjoining lot and grabbed a lightpole for balance as he swung around the corner. His other hand clutched the waistband of his baggy dungarees to keep them from slipping below his knees and tripping him up. It looked comic but he sure could fly.

I absorbed all this in a fraction of a second. I holstered the .38, grasped the top of the window frame in both hands, and swung feet first through the opening, taking out the rest of the glass from the edges and tearing my suit coat. It was an eight-foot drop to the ground, but I bent my knees to dampen the impact and broke into a sprint before my nerve endings could get word to my brain. I hurdled an exploded trash bag filled with dirty diapers, did the stripper's turn around the light pole, fixed on a flash of pale shirttail rounding the corner of a house, and pounded the sidewalk in pursuit.

He had youth and speed, but my legs were longer and I was desperate for his story. I fell back on jungle training, measuring my breathing and letting the noise of my soles slapping the concrete put me in a trance where fatigue and the sawing in my throat and the pain in my side had no meaning.

I caught a break when he changed directions to duck through a hole in the bottom of a chain-link fence barely large enough to admit a muskrat; I grasped the top with one hand and vaulted on over, gaining a couple of yards. If I'd had time to think I couldn't have managed it. There was nothing inside the fence, which seemed to have been erected only to prevent cars from cutting across the corner of the empty lot to avoid a stoplight. Cockleburs snatched at my socks, a solitary feral sunflower nearly as tall as I was smacked my shoulder with its big heavy head. I ran, and fed on running.

The small figure lost ground turning its head to see if I was still behind. A young, mixed-blood face, male, twisted with terror. He accelerated; so did I. I found a higher gear I hadn't known I had.

We crossed a couple of streets and barreled through a service station, startling the attendant into dropping the aluminum pole he was using to hike the prices on the tall sign. He thought the revolution had come. We charged across a parking lot. I lost a few steps galloping between cars as my quarry pounded up over the hoods and roofs and down the trunks. I couldn't do that without caving something in and falling farther behind.

We passed pedestrians: old women in black coats with head scarves, young blades brushing up their boulevard strut, a couple in matching warm-up suits out jogging, a kid carrying a big padded envelope reading addresses. It was one of those neighborhoods that is going from something toward something else. We got some startled gasps, but mostly they just made way. Street theater is a daily event.

In a chase, it's the one being chased who plots the course. When a cab pulling an empty flatbed trailer shifted down to obey a yellow light, my witness turned at a right angle, leapt up onto the bed, and off the other side. I let my momentum do the thinking and followed. Just then the driver decided he could make the light after all and shifted back into second. I lost balance as he accelerated and tumbled off the far edge on my hip. On the dismount I managed to throw my weight forward and avoid slipping under a wheel.

I lost my subject for a second, but heard the *rat-a-tat-tat* of his footsteps when I held my breath and took off after the noise. He came into view weaving around a pile of broken furniture in front of an apartment house.

Passing the pile I pressed two fingers to the side of my

neck. The Surfaris were playing "Wipeout" in my carotid. In the pursuit of my profession I'd been shot, beaten, cold-cocked, drugged, and threatened with death. I had my own parking space outside Traumatic Care. It would be a good joke on a lot of bad people if it was a heart episode that took me. I ran as if I was the one being chased.

A commercial zone came up. He thundered down a covered wooden walkway attached to a hotel under construction—in a city that attracts fewer visitors than the Beirut Bob Evans, clearly a graft job—past an adjoining parking structure, and through a bus stop. We foiled at least two drug transactions and a possible negotiation for immoral services; I know I got an ungrateful gesture from a young woman in spray-on shorts and high-heeled waders. At this point I was inhaling razor blades.

The boy—it was a boy, I knew that much now—was nearing the end of his rope. I figured he'd spent some energy early on, doing whatever it was he'd been doing in Johnny's house when I'd interrupted him, and stumbling upstairs to hide. But I was closer to the end of mine. I was slowing despite myself, doubling my investment and getting only half the return. My legs began to wobble.

I got lucky—I thought. A full-time street recycler in a canvas bucket hat and navy peacoat came out of an alley to the left, pushing a shopping cart piled high with cans and forty-ounce bottles squarely into the boy's path. The boy lost ground swerving to avoid collision and I lunged, reaching for a handful of jersey jacket, but he grasped the cart by the end and heaved it over onto its side. I hit the cascading returnables and fell across the cart, barking my ribs on the steel frame. The boy bodychecked the pilot of the cart into a one-legged dance to catch his balance and was gone down the alley.

I dragged myself vertical, glass crunching underfoot, and got an earful from the man; judging by the wealth of his vocabulary, he'd come by the navy coat honestly. I hooked my wallet and waved a white flag. The five-dollar bill vanished even faster than the boy, but the old sailor lost interest in me as he stooped to salvage what he could of his cargo.

I did some salvaging of my own as I limped back the way I'd come, blowing like a horse and probing my rib cage for breaks. What had happened didn't exactly match my recurring nightmare, but there's no science in prescience. Maybe it would stop.

The house was as I'd left it, the piece of siding still ajar. It was only forty years old, but government construction ages seven to the year. Father Marquette might have hung his cassock inside.

Time hadn't been any kinder on me. My lungs ached and my sweat was growing cold, wrapping me in a clammy shroud. My pulse had slowed to a drum roll. A family of porcupines had crawled backward out of my throat and someone was running a blowtorch up and down my leg in a steady rhythm. My breath came in short pants, like Mickey Mouse. I was running out of metaphors to describe my condition. There's nothing like a brisk workout to release the poet in us all.

I was pooped. And my day was just beginning.

Once again I entered behind my gun. But the stillness inside was complete. As I was putting away the weapon, the front sight snagged in something. The flap pocket of my suit-coat hung in a triangle with the lining exposed. I frowned at it and started inventory.

Nothing about the position of the upside-down wheelchair had changed, but I saw now it was the one Johnny used. The scabbard he'd fixed to the side to socket his rifle was empty. Something scraped the floor when my toe touched it and I recognized the single-shot with the slim pistol grip designed for an adolescent hand, an antique model marketed to boys who wanted to grow up to be Teddy Roosevelt; in Detroit, scraphounds excel at recovering percussion weapons from every chapter in history. Johnny was small, built to wriggle through ducts and basement windows. It was no wonder he'd kept the rifle. I bent down to pick it up and saw a foot in a size six-and-a-half combat boot.

It was at the end of a leg sheathed in faded camo. I straightened back up and set the chair on its wheels and found the other leg, bent the wrong way at a right angle, as thin as its mate with the material draped over the atrophied muscles. The rest of him lay twisted over onto his face. The chair had covered him almost completely. He looked like a sock puppet, without any support structure inside.

The knitted watch cap had slid from his shiny shaved head. There was a dent in the skull that reminded me of the golden cherub, only in his case it was starred like caved-in glass. Blood and black cerebral fluid had settled into the cracks, making a pattern. The skull wasn't the only thing broken and I stepped outside quickly to gulp fresh air. When the nausea settled I went back in to finish what I'd started.

TWELVE

I t had been no random working-over. I counted at least three blows that would have done the job. Probably there were more; certainly there were more, from the rag-and-sawdust way he lay at my feet. Man wasn't intended to survive as an invertebrate. But the city pays people to record every point of impact, and when I turn over a body and it responds like a sack of broken china my curiosity is satisfied. I had no doubt, from what Mary Ann Thaler and Lieutenant Hornet had said, that Reuben Crossgrain and Johnny Toledo had run into the same human threshing machine.

His skin felt cool, but I was still overheated from the foot race, so my internal thermometer was on the fritz. He might or might not have been dead long enough to clear Gale Kreski of his murder. The number I'd called less than thirty minutes earlier belonged to Kreski's shop clear across town, but these days you never know when you've been shuttled to someone's cell. I had only his word he'd been waiting on a customer. That might have been a stall to turn on the radio in his dash and cover the ambient noise of an automobile in motion. So far he was the only person I'd met on this case who'd given me reason to think he was trained in martial arts.

On the other hand, what did I know? Anyone with a buck and a half to rent *Fists of Fury* knew how to strike the right pose in a bluff.

I didn't know why Kreski would want Johnny dead. But then I didn't know why Johnny was dead at all. Once you'd made the decision to live on the dark side of the moon, all your friends were infernal angels at best. I'd lost the 10K to the only person who might be able to tell me what had happened and who had made it happen. The boy was a whiz at track and field, but he lacked the ballast necessary to inflict so much damage, even on someone stuck in a chair. He was even smaller, for one thing, and at a glance I saw nothing nearby that was bloody enough to have been used as a bludgeon.

Theft is always good in a pinch. It rates right up there among the Commandments for a reason. The dead man had been sitting—literally, sitting—on a modest fortune in reclaimable metal. The people who paid good money for it weren't issued hot lists, unlike pawnbrokers, and never paid attention to VINs or serial numbers, only scales. But if theft was the motive, whoever had gone to all this trouble had left most if not all of the plunder behind. He wouldn't scare off easily. Conquering panic is one of the first lessons they teach in the dojo. I didn't know if the cherub had toppled off its stand during the beating or in a hurried search afterward. It wasn't talking without the advice of counsel.

A search was good; I liked a search. It would be a second thing tying the two killings. I hadn't really counted on Johnny calling me in the event he came into possession of those TV boxes. He was a fence, not a snitch. He'd convert them into cash the old-fashioned way, by turning hot goods around at a profit.

I put a cigarette between my lips, just to see if I could manufacture enough saliva to make it stick, and buried my hands in my pockets. "You made your mark, Johnny," I said. "That's the measure of a man. They'll notice you're gone when the scavenging drops twenty percent."

I took out my cell, entered 911, and paused with my thumb on the SEND button. I remembered he had a cell.

One more sophisticated than mine, that took pictures, kept a record of incoming calls, and stored frequently called numbers for one-touch access. It would be the Rosetta Stone that unlocked most of his secrets. I put mine away and knelt to go through his pockets.

It was an awkward business because I had my hand wrapped in a handkerchief. I wasn't concerned about leaving fingerprints. Someday, some egghead will develop the technology to lift them off fabric, provided he doesn't abandon fingerprinting entirely for DNA or some other sexy new science. The handkerchief helped me avoid direct contact with nasty damp spots. There is no dignity in death, just social embarrassment.

At length I sat back on my heels and used the handkerchief to mop my palms. He hadn't the cell on him, which was promising. It wouldn't have been in his pocket while he was using it, either before the beating or during it. And he hadn't called the law, partly because he was Johnny Toledo and partly because if he had I'd be up to my neck in it by now. Whoever he had called might have heard something.

I got up and made a quick reconnoitre. I hadn't the luxury of being methodical; as orderly as they were, a thorough sifting of all those piles needed a week. I inspected the wheelchair for handy pockets, groped inside the rifle scabbard to the bottom. No cell. I was prepared to assume it wasn't there.

That was promising, too, because it meant the killer might have taken it with him when he left. This was professional work, and pros don't take souvenirs unless leaving them behind is impractical.

Johnny Toledo had called someone on his cell within minutes of his death.

I gave one to the kid I send for hot dogs so he can send back pictures, he'd said. *I can't make him understand what's wrong with turkey franks.*

I knew who "the kid" was, within the narrowest margin of doubt. I didn't know his name, but I could pick him out of a lineup. I just couldn't outrun him.

THIRTEEN

J ohnny Toledo had subsisted almost entirely on a diet of
frankfurters, obtained for him by the kid he'd given a cell
phone to, or so he'd said. There were several markets within
reasonable walking distance of his house. I went to the wrong
one first, a small square celery-green block building operated
by a bald Hungarian who spent the entire interview chopping
the heads and feet off dead chickens with a monster cleaver.
He spoke only at the end: "No."

"No, you never saw him, or no, you won't answer?" I asked.
"No."

A woman placing items in a handbasket smiled at me as
I was heading for the door. She had a round, pleasant face,
virtually wrinkle-free, but her hair, worn loose to the shoulders, was iron gray and she had the red, swollen hands that
come from a million scrubbed pots and pans. "Don't let
Laszlo upset you," she said in a low voice with a light accent.
"He's lived here as long as I have, and he's never forgiven the
neighborhood for changing."

"Have you?" I was being polite.

"I take things as they come. He was a child when he left the old country. He doesn't remember how bad things can get. You said the boy you're looking for is black?"

"Hispanic too, I think. Maybe Arab." I gave her the same description I'd given the shopkeeper.

"He sounds like someone I've seen around. He always wears that same red jacket."

"In here?"

"Oh, no. Black people don't patronize places where they know they're not welcome. I don't know how Laszlo stays in business." Her smile grew doubtful. "Are you with the police?"

"I'm not against them." I was carrying my torn suit coat. I got my ID out of it.

She put on a pair of glasses on a silver chain to read. "Gracious. I didn't know there were any of you left."

"Overhunting. We're protected now." I put it back. "The boy's not in trouble. I just want to ask him some questions for my client."

"You might try the Vietnamese."

"Where are they?"

"They own the party store on the corner of Greenfield. They have the best goat cheese in town, or I wouldn't walk that far. I think that may be where I've seen him. He wears that same red jacket, winter and summer. When it's hot he ties it around his waist. I don't think he has a home to store his clothes in."

"Greenfield's a hike." I hadn't drawn the circle that wide.

"Not for him. He runs in, he runs out. Never walks, only runs. I wish I had that kind of energy."

So did I.

I thanked her. "Why do you shop here if Laszlo's such a grouch?"

"I don't have any choice. He's my son."

It may not have been too far to run, but it was too far to walk. I was down to my last two Vicodin.

I'd parked Ernst Dierdorf's rolling bomb down the street from Johnny's. It had no antipollution equipment to steal, and in any case the block in front of the home of a known receiver of stolen goods is a psychological no-man's zone. Even so, someone had left smears on the passenger's side window peering in at the Stone Age sound system before moving on to brighter prospects. He'd missed the forest for the trees, so maybe there was something to be said for the unfinished paint job.

As I got in I gave the house a glance. No prowl cars yet. Johnny might stay right where he was until the cops came around to ask about those missing catalytic converters. The people he did business with weren't about to do the department any favors and if the boy hadn't called them by now he never would. I made a mental note to tip them off the next time I was near an anonymous pay phone; right after they tracked one down and told me where it was.

My route went past one of the hot dog sources I'd plotted out originally. I stopped there first. The Vietnamese might have been God's gift to lovers of goat cheese, but you can get wieners anywhere.

It was a pump-and-pantry station with height measurements marked on the chromium door frame so the security camera could give the cops a better description of armed robbers going in and out. The man behind the counter was a chiseled-face Sikh in a powder-blue turban and an immaculate beard. His English was better than mine, but I don't get much chance to polish my grammar. He listened to my pitch as he changed tapes in the cash register, then nodded.

"Yes, he comes in sometimes. There is no Arab in him. I am thinking he is Mexican. He has a cellular telephone. Once it rang and I heard him say, 'This is Luis.' "

"Do you know where he hangs out?"

He shook his head, banged down the hood of the register. "He always pays cash, so there is no need to ask for an address. I doubt he has one."

"When was he in last?"

"Yesterday, perhaps the day before. He bought a package of frankfurters. Frankfurters is all he ever buys."

"Can you think of any reason why he might leg it all the way over to Greenfield to buy them?"

"I cannot. I always order many so I never run out. They are a staple of this neighborhood, a source of inexpensive protein. I know this establishment to which you refer. The owners overcharge for everything. No one would travel that far on foot just to purchase frankfurters." He lowered his tone, although I was the only one within earshot. "They sell cigarettes alone at a discount, which they obtain from the Indian reservation near Mount Pleasant. They pay no tax, so they charge no tax. I do not support tax fraud."

"Does this Luis smoke?" If he did I intended to switch to his brand. He had wind enough for the Big Bad Wolf.

"I have never seen him do so. He probably sells them on the street for a profit."

I couldn't think of any more questions. That part of town

seemed a narrow slice of the universe to contain two such different merchants as Laszlo and the Sikh.

"Thanks. I'd appreciate it if you called me on my cell the next time he comes in. There's another one of these in it if you can fake a broken register or something and hold him ten minutes." I laid a twenty-dollar bill on the counter with my card on top of it.

He picked up the card between a pair of slim elegant fingers and slid it between two buttons on the front of his white tunic. The twenty stayed behind. "Give it to the boy when he answers your questions, or even if he does not. Someone so young should not have to spend every night on the street."

I took it back and left, starry-eyed. In two days I'd encountered a pawnbroker and a convenience-store clerk who were working in war zones and willing suckers for a hard-luck story. Maybe things were looking up for the city after all.

The party store on the far corner of forever brought me back down to earth with a bang. When I entered the double-wide trailer on a block foundation there was a heated argument going on and it continued as I browsed the shelves of plastic funnels and bags of chips. The customer was Vietnamese, the proprietor was Vietnamese—tall for a Southeast Asian, with black hair in a stiff crew cut—and the topic under discussion appeared to be the denomination of the bill that had changed hands and the amount of change the customer had coming. Some things are transparent in any language.

In a little while more change appeared, accompanied by a rattle of shrill Vietnamese on the part of the counterman. The other stuffed it in his pocket and stamped out without further discourse, jerking open the door with a clatter of bells and letting it coast shut with a pneumatic hiss. Neither man gave the impression of satisfaction. The register drawer slammed home.

This one called for an entirely different tactic. I'd left my coat in the car, but had kept the imitation leather folder with my license and the county star. I snugged up the knot of my tie and approached the counterman with a businesslike step, forcing the bad leg to keep up with its mate. I folded the ID out of sight, flashing the metal, and asked him in rusty Vietnamese if he spoke English. I'd left most of what I'd once known clear on the other side of the world.

"My wife. Little." He'd changed his attitude like a reversible coat, showing me the respectful side. He was old enough to have emigrated not long after Saigon fell; uniforms and official credentials called for restraint. "Luy!" It sounded like "Louie," and for an unreasonable split second I thought he'd said "Luis," but then a woman came in from the back and I made the spelling adjustment in Western characters.

This was the other half of the couple. She was shorter than her husband by half a foot and broader around the waist by the same measurement, a round little creature wearing a green apron over a print dress with her black hair bound behind her head and streaked with gray. Her face was crumpled like old cellophane but I placed her age close to his, solidly in the middle. Black eyes glittered in folds of skin that angled down away from her nose. I read her expression the same way I read Sanskrit.

A swift exchange took place between them that left me in the dust. She seemed to speak in a mixture of different dialects, souvenirs of dozens of relocations before the big one. I'd put away the badge, not wanting to press my luck. She met my gaze. "Yes?"

I said, "We picked up a boy a little while ago trying to lay off cigarettes from the reservation on an undercover officer. He says his name is Luis and that he bought them here."

I might have told her I was selling subscriptions to *The Mekong Gazette* for all the information seemed to have affected her. She translated for her husband, who gave me a little more, paling a shade beneath the tobacco-ivory of his face. He said something in which I clearly heard *Luis.*

"Not know that name," she said. "Not sell illegal cigarettes." She swept a hand toward cartons of Viceroys and Lucky Strikes on shelves behind her.

"I can come back with a warrant."

This time she didn't consult. Her chin rose. "Find nothing."

Her pidgin was broad even for summer stock. It can be an impenetrable screen. I let a little silence crawl past on its knees and elbows. A customer came in and went straight to a glassed-in cooler where the cheese was kept. It wasn't Luis. I blew air and tugged loose my tie. I tried to look tired. It wasn't hard.

"Yeah, we were pretty sure he was stalling us. We had to run it out. It's Arabs working the smuggled-smokes circuit these days, not you people. They funnel the profits direct to Al-Qaeda."

"Ah." The magic name sparked a dual reaction. The wife had followed the rest well enough, the first slip in character she'd shown. She nodded animatedly. "We good Americans. God bless U.S.A."

I nodded too, gravely. We were pulling each other's leg so hard it was a miracle we didn't all stand lopsided.

"He seemed to know your establishment," I said. "Maybe you've seen him in here, maybe with somebody, or maybe you heard him mention a name, someone he hangs with." I gave her the boy's description. I'd repeated it so many times it didn't sound like him anymore.

"Hang?"

"Keeps company with. What we call known associates. Criminal types mostly. Somebody's financing him—giving him money to buy the merchandise he sells on the street. It isn't terrorists because we froze all their assets." I was plagiarizing now from Mary Ann Thaler. "If we can link him to some high-profit racket, we'll be halfway home to taking those cigarettes out of circulation."

I was laying it on with a paver, and there were holes in it you could drive through with a wagon and team, but she didn't even ask what a character with a county badge was doing monkeying around with national security. Well, no one knew anymore where the boundaries were. For her and her husband, here was a chance for a diversion while they found a safe house to store the contraband.

Every penny they skimmed off the tobacco tax went into their own personal lockbox, not the Middle East. Everybody wants cheaper cigarettes. You don't have to turn coat to fill the demand. They had another rapid parlay, both of them nodding like they were bobbing for apples. She cut him off in midstream and turned her glittering eyes on me.

"Johnny Toledo. Scrap man, very bad."

Velly bad, yes; and velly good. It was progress, if only a little. Luis was the boy I wanted. I grunted; I was barn-theater material myself.

"We know Johnny, all right. That wheelchair hasn't slowed

him down any. We'll check him out. This Luis have a last name? Homeland Security says we can't book 'em as John Does no more. The ACLU makes a stink and we have to let 'em go." I almost blushed saying it. Just because someone drops her verbs and articles doesn't mean she's more gullible than a native.

It flew, though; it was Homeland Security that closed the deal. The two words drifted to the top of the torrent she aimed at her husband, who paled some more. For them it was the NVA, the SS, and the KGB all rolled into one. They were very anxious to get rid of me. If they weren't so afraid of the Patriot Act they'd have stopped to consider why they were expected to know the full name of a casual customer.

"Luis Quincy Adams," she said. "Like sixteenth president."

I repeated it. It sounded too made-up not to be genuine.

"You're good citizens," I said. "You might want to think about studying a little more American history before you take the test."

We parted with anxious smiles all around. Mine was tight with shame. I didn't like that it was as easy as that, or what I'd used to make it so.

I wound up the Buick and shipped off. I wondered if Barry Stackpole's computer voodoo could dig up contact information on Luis Quincy Adams. There weren't likely to be two people in Detroit with that name. It wasn't the kind of alias that would occur to someone living in the inner city.

While I was waiting in an inside lane for a light to change, Luis of the Flying Feet slouched through the crosswalk, hands in the pockets of his red jersey jacket. His head of brown curls stirred casually in the wind. Nothing about him said he'd run the race of his life within the hour. I resented him for that.

I gave him the corner, then wheeled around it across the outside lane, nicking the light, but for once not causing inconvenience for other motorists; I'd seen block parties with more auto traffic. I felt light of heart. Second shots don't come along every day, and now I had horsepower.

FOURTEEN

I had the speed now, but he had the agility. I had to play this one with surgical gloves.

For all the ease of his slouching gait, Luis was spooked, which on top of the necessary caution that went with his everyday circumstances gave him second sight; he looked around frequently. So far, though, he was thinking in terms of pedestrians. That would change the moment he suspected I'd switched to a different method of transportation. I gave him a full block, cruising at a walking pace to avoid overtaking him and forcing him into evasive action.

It needed better planning. Few people in Detroit pay much attention to posted speed limits, and fewer still drive very far below them. Most who do are trolling for a drug deal or a few moments of companionship or setting up a drive-by shooting.

When the traffic picked up a little I put on more gas. I was counting on the protection of the herd to pass him and set a trap.

As I drew abreast of him I turned my head the other way, as if I were looking for an address. What I saw out the tail of an eye made me envious. He hadn't even sweated through his jacket, on a mild day with a marathon behind him. He did glance at the car, and I had a few choice names for Ernst Dierdorf for not setting me up with a beige Volare or something similarly invisible. A car town is a car town is a car town. Boys are born there with a full knowledge of cylinder displacements and compression ratios; they recognize a muscle car no matter how much it needs paint, and they pay attention to it and who's driving. But as he came into the rearview mirror he'd gone back to studying people on the street. The flushed face he'd seen chasing him must not have borne much resemblance to the one behind the wheel.

Halfway up the next block I found a loading zone in front of a textile warehouse and slid into the curb. I'd parked the .38 in the glove compartment when I'd taken off my coat. I got it out, dragged myself slowly over the gearshift knob in its console, and hunched down in the passenger's seat, resting my other hand on the door handle.

There followed an anxious wait. I didn't have a mirror on that side, and wasn't sure how much time to give him before deciding he'd reversed directions or stepped through a doorway.

I'd about given up on him when he came inside my periphery, hands still in his pockets and moving at that deceptively slow clip. I knew from experience he had the reflexes of a rabbit. I let him have two beats, then flung open the door.

It caught him by surprise. He unpocketed his hands and threw them out in front to brace himself against the top of the frame and prevent a collision. I buried the muzzle of the revolver in his ribs.

"A moment of your time, Luis."

The Olympics needed him; the Tigers could use him at first base. He shucked out of his jacket in less than a second, slung it around my gun hand, and jerked it to the side. I'd had the foresight not to rest my finger on the trigger or I'd have fired a stray shot into God knew who. By then he'd left his wardrobe behind and was running full tilt down the sidewalk without a backward glance. Doing that had cost him ground before. He learned as fast as he moved.

I swirled my arm free of the jacket, threw myself back at the helm, banging an ankle on the shifting cane, and hit the accelerator, spinning the wheel away from the curb. My rear tires spun, snatched hold of the asphalt, and catapulted the car forward, drawing an answering shriek of rubber from an SUV that had been coming up in that lane. By the time the driver thought to stand on his horn I'd cleared twenty yards.

When Luis spun right on his heel into a side street, I was ready for him, bumping over the curb and fishtailing for traction with all the street signs facing the wrong direction. I lost the rest of my luck when a police cruiser came into view crossing at the end of the short one-way block. It hesitated, then threw on its lights and siren and turned my way.

I was driving a vehicle that wasn't registered in my name. Sorting it out would take most of the day and void whatever free hand I had. Whoever had pinned a tag on me, Thaler or Hornet, would be back on my rear bumper with an open tail I couldn't shake with a shovel. I threw the Buick into reverse before the wheels stopped rolling, forcing a gasp and an ominous shudder from the transmission. The car wasn't built that would put up with much of that. I roared backward around the corner, one arm on the back of the seat and watching through the rear window, dead into the path of the same

SUV I'd made acquaintance with previously. The driver was still shaken from the earlier incident, picking his way forward nervously, and had time to swing out of the way into the opposite lane. No other cars were coming in either direction, but it was a costly day for Goodyear. I banged into first and set fire to some more.

Motor City cops are almost impossible to lose; they share the same DNA with their units. I never put more than a block between us, and they would be on the air for help from up ahead. I had stop sticks in my future and a bad time with the license review board in Lansing.

I was going in the direction of home. The plan was to make it far enough around some handy corner to ditch the car and take off on foot. They'd trace it to OK Towing & Repair, but Ernst had more pull with the police department than I had. He'd once told me he'd agreed to replace the windshield on an official car and lose the record; something about a precinct commander accidentally blowing a hole through it when he was taking his sidearm off cock. With brass in the picture they might predate an auto theft report. They might even forget to process fingerprints.

As a plan it was worse than Ruby Ridge, but it was all I had, and I wouldn't have time to mop up before bailing out.

Lucky breaks are rare, and cost you all the ones you have coming when things turn bad. The old woman in the market and the Sikh in the convenience store had broken the budget. I made the turn I needed to set up the plan and slammed into the trunk of a neutral-colored, anonymous-looking sedan that was moving slowly, looking for the private detective who'd given it the slip that morning.

I wasn't belted. The steering column hit my chest with the

force of a three-pounder. My lungs didn't have the chance to reinflate before the police cruiser screamed around the corner and struck the Buick from behind.

The bad dreams would stop now for sure. But what good are they if they don't protect you from what's going to happen anyway?

FIFTEEN

hey were waiting for me when I came back from X-ray.

Not the officers who'd rear-ended me; I'd been told they were still being treated for cuts and abrasions and under observation for possible concussion.

Not the two men I'd rear-ended, either; one was a candidate for whiplash, the other had a broken nose caused by overeager deployment of an air bag. Hospital staffs are hell for gossip.

No, these were two different officers with the Detroit Police Department, uniforms from Traffic Safety armed with notebooks to pump me for details about the accident. They were polite and businesslike. They always are at that stage of an investigation. Cops only yell and throw chairs at persons of interest on TV, where the forty-minute guarantee of a conviction never fails. I told them everything I could—about the accident. No murders came up during the conversation.

I had a sore chest and a stiff neck, and someone was studying a set of eight-by-ten glossies for evidence of broken ribs and a cracked sternum. Sometimes the risk is equal even when the basic safety equipment isn't in place.

They thanked me and left, but lying on my gurney in a toy paper gown I was aware of a lingering presence outside the door of the room. They were waiting on orders whether to charge me with fleeing and eluding, reckless driving, reckless endangerment, and driving the wrong way on a one-way street. Nothing would be overlooked when personnel were involved.

I should have been concerned, and I was, but only on a remote level. I was shot full of painkillers, and for the first time in what seemed months the ghost of the slug that had torn through my leg was in hibernation. I could use a smoke. One of Luis Quincy Adams' Indian-reservation cigarettes would do.

Lieutenant Hornet came in looking like a fat kid with an ice cream cone. He had on a sport coat and slacks that matched in everything but color, texture, and style. His shirt puckered where the seams were fused rather than stitched and his necktie had run out of steam just above the fourth button after the lap around his neck. "You look like—"

"I was shit by a pigeon," I said.

"Hey, that's not bad."

"I got it from one of yours. The one who put me in this mess."

"Well, we all got to take responsibility for our own messes. You got a jim-dandy. We can bung you up for ninety days rock-bottom, then kick it over to the state police. Hope you like security work."

"A private license isn't as brittle as you think."

"It breaks pretty easy with two law enforcement agencies tugging on both ends."

"We'd be holding this conversation somewhere else if you and Thaler had given me the two days you promised."

"You'll have to take that up with her. That car you creamed is registered to Washington."

"I figured that. They're easier to ditch than Detroit cops."

"As who knows better than you. Why try ditching 'em at all? You turned a misdemeanor traffic citation into a string of felonies when you stomped on the gas."

"I was overdue for a haircut. The barbershop closed at five."

"I think it had to do with that heap you were driving. We traced it to a garage operating outside the law."

"Talk to anyone there?"

"Question part's mine."

"What's it say on the books about borrowing a car from a friend?"

"You got no friends. If you had one when you borrowed it, you sure don't now. That Buick looks like a beer can that went through the crusher. You know, the law in Michigan says when your car rear-ends another, you're at fault for not maintaining control of your vehicle. It can be sitting in the middle of the lane just over a hill and you're still on the hook for it. It don't make no sense, but it's the law."

"Did you ticket the cops who rear-ended me?"

"Not my department. That beat-up Olds of yours turned up at the same garage. You want to enlighten me on that?"

"A man leaves his car at a repair place and drives off in another. Why don't we find a detective and ask him what he makes of it?"

But he was in too good a mood to needle. "That's some service for a chop shop. The owner apparently delivered the loaner to your door, or close to it—the Buick wasn't seen—and picked up your car and drove it to the garage. He was followed there under the impression it was you driving."

"Show me one conviction for receiving and selling stolen vehicles or parts at OK Towing that makes it a chop shop. Show me one arrest."

"Not the point. You and this Dierdorf character are both guilty of interfering with federal officers in the performance of their duties."

"In that case I ought to be having this conversation with the feds. Next time you wander this far outside your jurisdiction, leave bread crumbs. Otherwise you'll never find your way back."

"Yeah, well, who knows where one leaves off and the other starts up anymore? We're still wrassling over why you spooked when that cruiser turned on its lights. Your hair don't look so shaggy to me."

"It's practically tickling my insteps."

"What were you doing in that part of town that was so important you couldn't wait for a street that was going your way?"

"I hear you can get good goat cheese there."

His face darkened. I'd found his range finally: Tell the truth, spark a vascular incident. I didn't get the chance to build on it, though. Mary Ann Thaler came in carrying a woven-leather bag over the shoulder of a brown suit.

"What possessed you to flee an officer of the law?" she said.

"I'm doing as well as can be expected. Thanks for coming to visit."

Hornet said, "I asked already. I'm handing it off to you."

"What were you doing in that neighborhood?"

"Why don't you and the lieutenant step outside? You can divvy up the script while I finish counting ceiling tiles. Who needs sleep? I've got morphine."

She glanced back at the closed door, then unshipped her bag and hung it on a visitor's chair. "What've you got?"

"Possible fractures. A sore neck for sure. I'll be making all right turns for a while."

"That will be a nice change from the usual zigzag. You know what I meant."

"I just got through telling Hornet I had another day and a half coming before you got to ask that question."

"Things have changed. It isn't the investigation it was when we struck that bargain."

"Things change fast. The ink isn't dry on our handshake."

"If I don't report back to the MacNamara Building with some answers, it won't be my case anymore. The next person who asks might not be so polite."

"He can't be worse than Hornet."

"Yeah, and you're Emily Post," he said.

I let him have that one. I was curious, and cautious. The opium made me more vulnerable than usual. If the change Thaler was talking about meant she knew there was a second murder, a slip on my part would put me on a shelf for a while as a suspect.

"We need to know what you turned up during that interesting excursion into the inner city," she said. "*I* need to know. I'm fighting for my little scrap of earth."

"Ladies first."

She said, "It doesn't work that way."

"Okay, Hornet first. Or does he know what's changed?"

"He does. This is a joint operation. Trying to split us up won't work."

I yawned. I didn't have to dig for it. "It'll have to wait. I'm getting pretty mellow."

"Buddy, there ain't enough dope."

She told him to shut up, without much conviction. She was concentrating on me. "You've got a buttload of charges outstanding, Amos. We can pick them when they're ripe or let them die on the vine. It's a brave new world, stuffed with options. Your choice."

"So it's Amos. That makes you the one who offers to fluff my pillow."

Hornet said, "Don't be so generous with them wes— Marshal. All you got's a personal injury case on behalf of your two people in the car. I got two cops in the hospital and ammo enough to put Walker on a bicycle from here to Easter."

"Deputy marshal." She spoke without inflection.

I closed my eyes. I was playing possum. I didn't figure I could be any less convincing than the one-thousand-and-first revival of a road show I hadn't liked when it played Broadway.

The joke was on me, but then it usually is. The padding under my back was a magic carpet. I went away from there. They were waiting when I woke up.

"He's back," said Thaler.

Hornet was standing at the window looking out. He wasn't so wide I couldn't see it was getting dark out. That reminded me I hadn't eaten since breakfast, and I never eat breakfast. I wondered when feeding time was. Thaler was sitting in the visitor's chair with her legs crossed and a bulky plastic bag on her lap. When the lieutenant came over I had the wild thought they were going to throw it over my head and smuggle me out through the laundry room.

She got up and transferred the bag to my lap. "Get dressed. The walls have ears, and the staff needs the gurney."

I untwisted the top and peered inside. It was a hell of a way to treat what was left of a good suit. My .38 wasn't in it, but then it wouldn't be. It would take paperwork to get it back from downtown.

"You keep telling me to put my clothes on, but I always sleep through the R-rated part. How'd my pictures turn out?"

"Better than you deserve," Hornet said. "One of my officers is still seeing double."

Thaler said, "No breaks or fractures. Are you Catholic?"

"Episcopalian. If you're planning my send-off."

"Episcopalians light candles, too. You should. How a man manages to total three cars and walk away, without a seat belt or an air bag to his name, would convert anyone."

"Where are we going?"

Hornet said, "Homicide."

Thaler said, "My office."

Once again they'd spoken together. The charm of their Frick & Frack was chipping off like paint from a trade-in.

"Let's make it my coop downtown," I said. "I've been neglecting the place lately."

The lieutenant shook his head. The displacement of flesh was equal to a snow shovel heaped with slush. "You'll like our new billet. They cleared us out of that shithole on Beaubien finally. It's at Grand River and Schaeffer. You can walk from there to your dump, seeing as how your car's still in the shop."

"The old second precinct." I shook mine. Little cartoon lightning bolts jumped from my neck. "I was there a few times back when it was local. They raced cockroaches during coffee breaks. The super in my building sprays once every two years."

"If he's more comfortable there," Thaler said, before he could continue the argument.

I sat up with the bag in my lap. Neither of them stirred. "My underwear's in here."

"Go ahead and put it on," she said. "I've got brothers."

"Me, too. Worthless sons of bitches that they are." A shred of pastrami fluttered between Hornet's front teeth.

The lieutenant at least turned his attention to the window while I shinnied into my shorts and pants under the foam blanket. Thaler watched me shuck the gown and thread myself into my shirt. The morphine was wearing off; all the muscles in my body rallied to its defense. I swung my legs over the side, put on my shoes, and stuck my socks in a pocket.

Thaler smiled. She looked even better when that happened, no matter what triggered it. "So how's this line of work treating you?"

"My mother wanted me to be a mailman, but I'm afraid of dogs."

The genteel, insurance-mandated custom of ferrying patients out in a wheelchair went unobserved. The ankle I'd barked on the Buick's shifting cane left me without a leg to favor, but I soldiered on; neither of them offered me an arm.

Her white government car was waiting in the lot. Hornet showed some humanity then, taking the backseat and letting me stretch my legs beside Thaler. When I sank into the cushions with a sigh I couldn't suppress, she reached inside her economy-size shoulder bag and handed me a foil square containing four Vicodin in blister wraps.

"They gave me these at the nurses' station. I didn't think to ask for water. Sorry."

"You don't put out this kind of fire with water." I poked out all four and chewed.

"You're supposed to take two in four hours," she said.

"Four in two is faster."

"It's your body." She started the car.

"Only until the University of Detroit gets it."

Hornet said, "I'm just sorry it'll be Narcotics takes you down."

The pills were kicking in when we got to the stairs to my office, in a building John Brown had passed when he'd come North looking for someone to underwrite the raid on Harpers Ferry. Rosecranz, the superintendent who'd been sweeping the floor at that time too, scarcely looked up at us as he cornered a dust bunny with his push broom in the foyer. He'd seen me stagger in under worse conditions and hadn't asked questions since Lenin was in rompers.

I tarnished my palm on the brackish brass of the bannister. At the top of the steep two flights I led the way through the half-liter reception room, which I never lock, shook out the key to the little isolation booth where I work out the problems of the universe, and held the door for my guests. That crack of Hornet's about Emily Post had cut me to the quick.

I let them find seats while I hoisted the window behind the desk. The air turned over like a sick old man in bed.

In the swivel behind the desk I opened the deep file drawer out of habit, then shut it when I remembered I'd stopped keeping a bottle there when I'd added pills to my daily vices. I regret most of my decisions.

"These walls are a foot thick, the way they used to make them," I said. "They don't have any more ears than a snake. Who's taking the investigation away from the U.S. Marshals?"

"We'll come to that." Thaler reached inside the woven leather shoulder bag. I'd been wondering about it. It was too big for her service piece and too small for a Saint Bernard.

SIXTEEN

he package was shaped like a brick, but smaller, and sealed
tightly in transparent plastic. She leaned forward to put it
on my desk. I let it sit for a second, then hefted it. It was
as pliable as bread dough and weighed a little more than a
pound. I slid it back her way.

"That's how the FBI nailed those dumb cops who substi-
tuted confectioner's sugar for the dope they took from the
evidence room," I said. "The real thing isn't that white. Not in
this town."

"Go ahead and taste it," said Hornet.

"I'm not a cadet facing initiation. I'd be tasting cocaine all
day long."

Thaler said, "No danger of that. Heroin has no taste."

I frowned at the brick. "I'm not buying it."

Hornet grinned. "You couldn't afford it."

"No one can." Thaler dived back inside the bag and thumped
another brick down next to the first. "Kilo even. There are two
more just like these. One's on its way to the FBI lab in Quantico, and this is as much as I'm authorized to carry around. If

my purse gets snatched I'm on my way to Leavenworth. It looks uncut, but no one can quite believe that. We'd need to requisition more zeroes to calculate its worth."

"You didn't find it on the street. Mexican brown's as good as it gets here. After the local dealers finished doing the Flamenco on a shipment like this it'd last a year."

"They ain't dancing," Hornet said. "Right there's the reason we got OD's stacking up like cordwood in the morgue. None of the locals has the experience to knock the horns off quality like this. The customers think they're pumping brown and it blasts through their veins like a comet."

"Only the mob has the organization to smuggle in that kind of cargo, but it wouldn't distribute it here. The economy won't support it."

"The guy we picked up with it lives in shelters and doorways."

I looked at Thaler to confirm what the lieutenant had said. She was busy scooping the dope back into her bag and didn't seem to be listening. Transporting that kind of valuables takes concentration.

"Rudy's the name," Hornet went on. "He's got more priors for petty than Bernie Madoff. Pair of officers in a city cruiser pulled over to talk to him last night when they spotted him walking down the street lugging a suspicious-looking box. He was so full of crack and Crown Royal he tried to climb aboard. He thought the unit was a bus."

"Why settle for crack when he had his hands on a fortune in high-grade horse?"

"He didn't open the box."

I was starting to see where the conversation was leading.

Not having anything in my stomach helped. All the circulation was going straight to my brain.

Hornet said, "He said he found it. We know he stole it. We don't know where from. He's clean now, screaming about getting swarmed by bees in holding, but he's blank on the last twenty-four hours. He ain't faking. The blood they drew at the clinic would light up the northwest side."

"That's where you picked him up?"

Thaler fastened the snaps on her bag. "That's why we want to know what you were doing there today."

"What kind of box was he carrying?"

"That's why they called me," said Hornet. "It was on the BOLO sheet."

"And that's why he called me. Rudy the street person had a dummy converter box under his arm with a manufacturer's plate on the back."

"MacArthur Industries," I said.

"Good guess. When they popped the box open at Thirteen Hundred, they found these inside." She patted the bag on her lap.

I frowned again. "Two kilos, that's a piece over four pounds. The box I held at Crossgrain's wasn't anywhere near that heavy. I remember thinking how light it was for all those wires and circuits."

"Components are mostly air, to keep the package from appearing too small for the price," Thaler said. "You told us Crossgrain had ordered the one he showed you first, to test it out. If it had turned out to be a dummy he wouldn't have ordered more. Depending on his honesty, if it came filled with drugs he might have gone into another business."

"He liked the one he was in. He'd have reported it." I stroked a burn crater on the desk with my thumb. "Someone made a mistake, mixed up his customers, and sent him a load of heroin when he placed his second order. He was out of town when someone came back to correct the mistake. When he showed up on TV still in possession of a box, that same someone paid another visit. Whoever it was couldn't be sure it didn't contain drugs, but in any case Crossgrain had to be eliminated before he could connect the police to his source."

"Even a criminal mastermind has a senior moment now and then," said Thaler. "The DEA wants this one. It would be a mistake if it gets it, because it's still national security. The mob doesn't have the capital. We're talking tending the poppy fields, refining the pollen, packaging and distribution across two hemispheres, and guarding it at every step. Those dregs they bring up from Mexico have about as much in common with this stuff as Chicken McNuggets and chateaubriand. It's Asian or Middle Eastern, possibly a combination of both, for backup in case of a government crackdown in one place or the other, or a UN air raid. The same mistake that put those boxes in Crossgrain's hands put this stuff on the streets of Detroit. Whoever pressed the wrong button probably isn't around anymore to interview. Ruthless methods, deep pockets. Same cast and play, different act."

Hornet said, "You got to hand it to them for balls, using one illegal smuggling operation as a front for another. A hell of a lot riskier one, to boot. Forgetting the rough characters you're competing with and every country in the world at war with what you're selling, some of that merch finds its way into the arms of your own employees, which dollars to dog shit is what happened in this case."

"A hell of a lot riskier," agreed Thaler, "and several hundred times the profit potential. What's in this bag would buy a nuclear warhead."

"I miss the mob," I said. "Serial killers. Street gangs. Cut-your-throat-for-a-nickel muggers. They're all Smurfs in retrospect."

"We got all them, too," Hornet said. "Every time something else comes along we slide 'em down a notch, like weekend box office receipts. Always something opening every Friday."

Thaler said, "This is as far down the street as this goes for now. If it gets around that this stuff is available, we'll have every dope-sniffing dog in the country at our throats in three days. The terrorists will break off the operation and start another from scratch. Something worse, maybe. It's taken us months to find out this much, and part of that was by accident. It may take years to bring us to this point on the next. Each mistake makes these drooling types smarter. We can't count on them slipping up again."

Hornet leaned forward to rest his hands on his knees and his belly between his thighs. "What were you doing violating a traffic ordinance just six blocks from where we picked up Rudy?"

"The truth, Walker. No half measures, lies of omission, wiseass punch lines. You don't want to be a hostile witness on Homeland Security's books. It's a lot easier to make the case for treason than it used to be."

So it was back to Walker. I was stroking the burn crater again when my office door opened and let in John Alderdyce, inspector in charge of Detroit Homicide. He wasn't the genie I'd been trying to summon.

His suits always looked fresh and well cared for, and he always looked tired. The hair he cropped close to his skull was a gray haze now and the lines from his nose to the corners of his mouth looked like guy wires erected to support the bags under his eyes. His head still looked as if it had broken off a quarry and his skin was so black it shone purple when the light struck the places where it was stretched over bone.

Mary Ann Thaler caught my unasked question. "I made a call when we were leaving the hospital. You were busy matching your feet to the steps."

Alderdyce remained standing, but then he had no other option but the floor. I usually had two more seats than customers, but today was a sellout. "I don't give a shit about some guy who wears his underpants on his head in some cave," he said by way of hello. "Not during business hours anyway. He's Thaler's job, not mine or Hornet's or I might add yours. I got dead junkies blocking doorways all over town. I can't take a chance some honest citizen'll trip and fall over one of them and break his neck. One more successful lawsuit against the city and then I'll have all the time in the world to give a shit. So what's the deal?"

I was outgunned. I struck a kitchen match off the crater and set fire to a cigarette, blew smoke at the dark spot on the ceiling. Following it up and out the open window was off the table.

I told them about both visits to Johnny Toledo's and what I'd found there the second time. I edited out one detail only. Luis Quincy Adams didn't have to exist for them just yet. Whoever had taken Johnny's cell phone had a complete record of his contacts. If it was his killer, he'd start with the last one called. Heavyweights are orderly and don't leave potential witnesses rattling around. Up to a bureaucratic point, I trusted John and Mary Ann to sit on a secret, but I didn't trust Hornet any farther than I could roll him uphill. He liked to hear himself talk and didn't pay much attention to whoever else was listening.

"I remember Johnny," he said. "He came under Homicide for a little when it looked like he wouldn't pull through after that spill he took from the high wire. I don't see Rudy for this. He isn't in shape to take a beating, much less dish one out. They say Johnny's inventory'd retire a modest man in style. We should look into who inherits."

Alderdyce was slouched against the door with his hands in his pockets, looking as languorous as Mount Hood. "Were you even going to report finding the body?"

"Sure. Even a scrap thief shouldn't be left to feed the rats."

"You was eager as hell," said Hornet, "wanted to do it in person. That's why you stumbled into that one-way from the wrong end. It don't explain why you rabbited when the police showed. They could've saved you the gas."

Thaler said, "You locals have plenty of time to turn him on the spit. If Rudy found this Toledo's house open and helped himself to what he found inside, maybe he saw something."

Hornet shook his head. "If he did, he blacked it out. All that shit he shoots has worn his brain as smooth as a door-knob."

"Hypnosis," she said. "Psychotropic drugs. If a computer geek can recover data from a crashed hard drive, a team of government shrinks can jump-start a user's memory."

"Maybe we should try them on Walker," Hornet said.

Alderdyce wasn't listening. He was watching me. "Who else did you talk to about those converter boxes?"

I thought of Gale Kreski. Even if Rudy had gotten his box from Johnny's the night before, I still wasn't sure Johnny had been dead long enough to consider Kreski a suspect, however much he knew about unarmed combat; his skin hadn't had the cold waxiness of a corpse that had lain in the same spot for hours. I kind of liked Kreski and didn't want to jam him up in another murder while he was defending himself against the charge in Guam. Also I thought I still had some use for him. I had no idea just what, but something other than sympathy kept me from saying his name.

The case wasn't about converter boxes anymore. It never had been, I knew now. When you have to throw someone to the wolves, make sure it's another wolf. "Eugenia Pappas."

"Who the fuck's Eugenia Pappas?" Hornet asked.

"Nick Pappas' widow." Alderdyce was still watching me. "She's kind of high-end."

"She stalled me with a promise to pump her husband's old contacts. Make what you want of that."

"Who else?"

"That's it. It's only been two days. I spent most of today on a gurney."

"Johnny spent longer on the floor," Alderdyce said.

Hornet wasn't satisfied; he had a curiosity to go with his appetite. "Failure to report a crime is a crime."

"Almost everything is now. A funny thing happened on my way to report it."

"You've got a cell. You could've done it from the scene and stayed to answer questions."

"I didn't see anything they wouldn't." Time was when it wasn't against the law to lie to a police officer, as long as you didn't sign anything. I hadn't studied the penal code lately but I supposed that had changed along with everything else when the hammer fell.

Alderdyce wasn't satisfied either, but he had the metabolism to withstand it. "It stinks that you didn't pull over for the cruiser. One ticket wouldn't bend your license."

"He had to get a haircut," Hornet said.

"In retrospect it was a lame thought," I said. "I was a little shook up."

"Murder suspects usually are. I say Johnny crawfished on your deal and you took away that squirrel rifle he totes around and beat him to death with it to make it look like what happened to your client."

Thaler shook her head. "Walker's a pain in the ass with a smart mouth and a couple of dozen other things I could name, but he isn't a life-taker. Even if he were, he'd know he couldn't match bare-handed work with a blunt instrument."

"We won't know they don't match till forensics gets it."

Alderdyce straightened away from the wall. "I've got papers to shuffle, and you two have reports to make. It's your collar," he told Hornet. "You holding him or not?"

"Not," said Thaler, before the lieutenant could open his mouth. "He gave us information we might not have had for a week. A few hours earlier would've been nice, but one more stubborn P.I. behind bars won't take an ounce of supersized heroin off the street. Cite him for reckless driving, if you like, but we've all got papers to shuffle."

"You're forgetting this is my investigation."

"So has downtown," Alderdyce said. "I got an e-mail this afternoon and confirmed it by phone. It's now a cooperative effort with federal and city authorities, with Justice calling the shots. Thaler's in charge, at least until DEA makes the case for jurisdiction."

She smiled, looking surprised. "I didn't know that when I called you, honest."

Alderdyce looked grimmer than usual. "Yeah. So far. Hornet's the only honest one in the room."

In a leap year, anything is possible.

SEVENTEEN

After they left, I righted the chair Hornet had tipped over scrambling out of it, made sure no one was lurking in the little reception room, then locked the door and called Eugenia Pappas. She answered herself.

She was silent while I explained the situation. I left in Reuben Crossgrain's murder, which was public property, but kept out Johnny Toledo's, which was not. I whittled things down to the bare fact that the cops were coming.

"I thought keeping confidences was why people hired people like you," she said when I finished. "Otherwise they'd just go to the institutions they pay taxes to support."

"You didn't pay me for my confidence, Mrs. Pappas. Anyway, it's an official investigation now. I just thought you'd like to know so you can set out milk and cookies for the visit."

"I suppose I should be grateful for that. I can't help thinking there was a better way to handle things."

"From where you're sitting, there's no doubt about that. From where I am there's plenty. Did Ouida find out anything about those converter boxes from your husband's people?"

"I thought you said the investigation had been taken away from you."

"It usually has been at this point. Since I didn't get the lay-off speech, I have to assume tacit approval of my cooperation, or at least a lower level of intolerance. In Washington it's called plausible deniability."

"And they called Nick a schemer. I can't help you, Mr. Walker. Ouida didn't return from lunch today and I haven't been able to reach her on her cell or at home. Frankly, I'm concerned. It isn't like her to take time off without leaving word. As a matter of fact, it isn't like her to take time off, period. I practically have to threaten her to use the two weeks' personal time I give her annually."

"Want me to check on her?"

There was a brief pause while she consulted her synapses. "I'd rather not give an employee's personal address to a stranger. At this point I'm still expecting to hear from her at any time."

"The offer's still good if you don't. Would you call me, or have her call me when she shows up?"

"That would be up to her. Thank you again for the information."

"I'm getting to be in the habit of handing out more than I gather in." But I was talking to an empty line.

I worked the plunger, then called Ernst Dierdorf at OK Towing & Reapir.

"*Ja?*"

"Oh, knock it off," I said. "I'm sorry about the Plymouth. Normally a new set of wheels lasts me more than half a day. Can I work out a payment plan? My capital these days is strictly lowercase."

"You don't think I'd let it off the lot without insuring it down to the valve caps, do you? I can make back four times that much parting it out. You didn't crack the block, and I can salvage most of the drive train. I expect to come out enough ahead on the deal to keep my lawyer in gold pen sets through December. Are you all right?"

"Someone thinks so. They kicked me out of the hospital." As I said it, I wondered if I'd been released at all. The whole business of my exit had felt like a bootleg job. I'd have bet a year's prescription that if I went back to see my records the screen would come up blank. A lump of ice touched my spine at the thought. If I didn't exist for Detroit Receiving, I could just as easily never have existed at all. It's one thing to walk around with a bull's-eye on your forehead, something else to go through life wearing a delete mark. The infernal angels overlooked nothing.

"Amos?"

"I'm here, Ernst. Much trouble with the authorities?"

"No more than always. When I saw they were going to follow me all the way back to the garage, I speed-dialed for legal help. It was on speaker phone when they came into the office. Apparently there's no law against swapping cars, even with a desperado like you. The advice was to answer no questions, but I told them honestly I had no idea where you were. They didn't hang around after that." An automatic tire spreader popped a rim in the background. It sounded like a pistol shot. "When we towed in that Plymouth, the paint chips on the front looked like the paint on that piece of shit they were following me in."

"They found me finally. Can I pick up my heap in the morning?"

"Anytime. You can pick up your suit coat, too. It got torn when you crashed the Plymouth."

"It was torn before. Thanks, and I'm sorry for the trouble."

"Just don't ask me for any more loaners. I'm in the auto business, not insurance."

I thanked him. When the receiver was in its cradle I let my hand rest on it for a moment, then picked it back up and dialed a taxi service to take me home. Even a day like that one had to end sometime.

While I was waiting, I broke open the safe and withdrew a few hundred from the emergency fund. I was running low on Crossgrain's case dough, tomorrow was Saturday, and without a car I wasn't sure I could get there before the bank closed at noon. I took the unregistered Luger from the compartment, inspected the magazine, and stuck the pistol under my waistband in the small of my back with a thick rubber band wound around the handle to keep it from slipping. It's a more cumbersome weapon than the .38 and the Germans who'd designed the action were too fond of moving parts, but the system is getting increasingly slow about returning perfectly legal firearms to their owners. Wearing it stiffened my spine in more ways than one.

I let the cab go in front of my house and emptied my pockets inside, laying the pistol next to my wallet and change. I hefted the cell and wondered if Mary Ann Thaler had snooped through the record of outgoing and incoming calls when she'd had my personal effects in her hands. The screen came up blank when I checked. I was in the habit of deleting stored numbers automatically, but there were ways and ways of retrieving such things. I didn't know how involved the process was or if she'd had time to put it in play. If she'd had, those converter boxes were closed to me, because she'd have all my contacts.

But as I'd said, the case wasn't about converter boxes anymore.

I stripped and stood in the shower ten minutes scrubbing off the stenches of hospital and authority. I had a green-and-purple bruise the size and shape of an ostrich egg on my chest from the steering column of the Plymouth, and when I peeled eight inches of treated adhesive from the right side of my rib cage I found a long red scratch where I'd scraped against broken glass climbing out the driver's window; the impact had sealed the doors shut. A tear inside my left cheek where I'd gnawed nearly through it smarted when my tongue touched it, so of course I couldn't stop touching it. No other topical damage at first inspection. I'd have bought a lottery ticket if I thought I had any luck left over.

My leg throbbed, but I was fresh out of pharmaceuticals. I got into a robe, poured a bracer without ice, and drank it down standing at the sink, like bicarbonate. It stung the torn spot inside my cheek and rang my head like a bell. I remembered then I hadn't eaten anything except my own flesh in twenty-four hours. I stuck a jar of peanut butter between two slices of bread and chased it with water from the Scotch glass. That began to sop up the effect, so I half filled the glass from the bottle, leveled it off with water, and carried it into the living room.

I didn't finish it. When the telephone rang I jumped in the armchair and didn't know where I was for two or three seconds. The antique clunkety-clock on the mantel showed past midnight. I'd been out an hour. I seemed to have stopped having the dream. Living it had been a poor trade.

The ringing continued when I lifted the receiver off the standard on the lamp table, and I realized it was my cell. I got to it in the bedroom just before it stopped on its own. Even so I hesitated half an instant with my thumb on the call button when I read the caller ID: J. TOLEDO.

"Hello?" I'd never hailed a ghost before. I thought maybe I'd dreamt the whole day there in the chair.

"You are looking for me, I think."

A young male voice with a strong Spanish accent. "Luis?"

"*Sí.*"

"Where are you?"

"What do you want?"

"Luis, I know you didn't kill Johnny."

"Then why do you chase me?"

"Because you know who did. Or have a good idea who did."

"I don't go to court."

"If you got my number off my card you know I'm not the police. You don't even have to talk to me if you don't want to. But I'm not the only one who's looking."

"I know this. How much you pay for what I tell you?"

"Enough to get you out of town till the situation changes, if it's good enough."

"Is good enough. You know Marcus Garvey?"

I thought at first he was offering me a lesson in black history, but then I remembered it was the name of an unlicensed liquor den a brisk walk from Johnny's hunting grounds; for Luis it would be a light sprint. Some former owner with a sense of humor had cast around for a patron saint and settled on an old-time black con man who'd bilked thousands from his own people promising to outfit a ship to return them to Africa in style.

"I know it," I said. "When can I meet you there?"

"Is where I'm calling from." The connection broke.

My taxi driver was three hundred pounds of muscle and suet in a bright dashiki with chrome grillwork on his teeth. He looked like a Buick towing a parade float. He shook his head when I gave him the address.

"I ain't black enough for that neighborhood this time of night. Nobody is."

"We're bringing a president along." I showed him a crisp fifty. "There's another one of these for the trip back if you wait."

"How long?"

"What do you drink?"

"Pure mineral water, with an Irish chaser."

"You can wait inside and I'll pick up your tab."

"And find my hack stripped when I come out? Bring me out a pint."

It was a tin Quonset hut built to protect construction equipment from thieves for a project that was never finished. If it had been any other kind of establishment, the current breed would've torn it apart starting with the privy roof and peddled it for scrap.

There were some cars lined up at the curb, but it wouldn't start doing real business until the licensed bars closed at two A.M., and then it would be mostly walk-in trade. I gave the driver his fifty. He snapped on his reading light to count the threads.

"You better give me the rest now. No white man's ever come out of there except feet first."

I grinned, tore another bill in half, and gave him a piece. "You can go through my pockets for the other one." I got out.

"Don't forget that pint." He tilted back the seat and settled into his folds of fat like a grizzly.

The roof didn't slant quite low enough to knock my head on but I stooped a little anyway; the pressure when I entered was enough to press wine. Groups were gathered at tables made from cable spools and pieces of plywood laid across liquor cartons, brows and cheekbones visible only in the light of three bare bulbs swaying above the bar, an old store display case someone had dragged from a landfill and boarded up where the glass was broken. The stingy illumination wasn't so much to save on electricity as to prevent customers from seeing the amount of wear on the labels of Jack Daniel's bottles filled with Old Spleenbuster.

The conversation level flattened out as I approached the bar. Behind it a photo of Marcus Garvey clipped from an ancient newspaper clung to the wall with yellowing tape. It had been taken before he exchanged his Queen's Admiral plumed hat and tunic for prison stripes on many counts of mail fraud. Mine was one of only two white faces present, but fortunately the other one belonged to Andrew Jackson. The bartender, a lean youth with pale freckles high on his brown cheeks, took the bill in trade for a small bourbon and a pint of what passed for Bushmill's for the cab driver. No change back represented the cover charge.

My eyes by now had adjusted to the gloom. I spotted Luis Quincy Adams sitting on a stool in a back corner with a scarred piano bench serving as a sort of coffee table at his knee. He'd

retrieved his red jersey jacket from where I'd disentangled myself from it, but I was a second making sure it was Luis. I'd
never seen him not in motion.

I hauled over a stray ladderback chair missing a few rungs
and sat down facing him, placing the glass and bottle next to
his longneck on the piano bench. "How old are you?" I asked.

He lifted his lip and dropped it over the mouth of his beer.
"Everybody's twenny-one in here."

I figured him for a tall twelve or a short fourteen. He was
built like a flexible straw with a mop of curly brown hair
stuck in one end. He had long lashes and a narrow rectangular jaw that would always make him look older than he was.

"Were you really named after a president?"

"I am named for my grandfather, Luis Tigrito, the greatest
matador in Argentina." He rolled his *r*'s and leaned heavily on
his *h*'s for *g*'s, a young man desperate to hold on to his accent.

"How old is he?"

"He would be sixty, but he liked too much his cigarettes."

"Too young."

"*Sí*." He nodded, pulling at the bottle.

"Not that. Argentina outlawed bullfighting under Perón."

"*Sí*. But the Little Tiger's grandfather taught him no other
skills. A thing does not go away because a law is passed."

"This place is proof of that. Ever run with the bulls?"

"It is my greatest wish."

"The bulls don't stand a chance."

He looked ten when he smiled. "You run fast for an old
man."

"You should've clocked me before I got shot."

He glanced at my clothes, a sweatshirt and jeans. "You
bring that gun of yours?"

"A different one. The other's day wear. I wasn't going to shoot you yesterday. I just wanted to slow you down long enough to talk."

"I wouldn' be here if I didn' think this."

"Who gave you my card?"

"Arab behind a counter. He said you have money for me."

I remembered the Sikh. "He wouldn't take any from me. And he wouldn't thank you for calling him an Arab."

"Is all the same when they tie that dishrag around their head. Lemme see the money."

The bourbon tasted like razor wire boiled in molasses. I clenched my teeth while it went down, then placed a folded hundred on the bench and stood the glass on top of it. "What were you doing at the shack?"

"I work for Juanito Toledo sometimes." He made him sound like a Mexican trumpet player. He kept his eyes on the bill.

"I guessed that. He said he paid a kid to fetch him hot dogs. He also said he gave you a cell phone to check in with and make sure you didn't buy turkey franks by mistake. His cell was missing when I searched. How much did you see?"

"His leg. I lift the chair and see he is dead. Then I hear you coming and put it back down. I go upstairs to wait until you leave."

"And if I'd left, what then?"

"Then I leave too. Is nothing to keep me."

"Nothing except Johnny's money stash, wherever it is."

He swigged beer, twitched a shoulder up and down. You had to come from old Spanish stock to shrug so eloquently. "Don' do him no good now."

"You can have the money, if the cops don't turn it first.

You're probably the closest thing he had to an heir. It's his cell I'm interested in. The only reason his killer would take it is if Johnny tried to call for help while he was being beaten. The killer needed the record of outgoing calls to find and eliminate a possible witness against him. You know 'eliminate'?"

"*Sí.*" He unwrapped his index finger from the bottle, making a gun of his fist, popped his lips.

"You'll wish he used a gun. You saw what he did to Johnny. He's still looking, Luis."

"I outrun him, I think."

"I almost caught you, an old man like me. The man who chopped Johnny to pieces did the same thing to an able man in good health a day or two earlier. He can run rings around me, and he won't stop until you're a bag of bonemeal."

The room started thumping like a boot in an automatic clothes dryer; the bartender had turned on Snoop Dogg on a ghetto blaster. For the next hour he'd charge entertainment tax. I leaned close to Luis and raised my voice a notch. "Johnny called you. I doubt you came back to help. I don't blame you for that, or for taking advantage of the situation to toss the place for cash. All I want to know is what did he tell you just before he got his lights blown out."

He shook his curls. "Not for no lousy hundred."

I opened my wallet, lifted my glass, and laid another hundred on top of the first.

"How many more of those you got?"

"I have to know what I'm buying." I put the wallet back on my hip.

He took his eyes off the bills then, looked around the room, tipped up his bottle until it gurgled empty like a downspout. No one was paying us any attention; when the bartender hadn't put up a kick over me, the show was over, at least until the place filled up in a little while and I started taking up room with my one little drink. Everyone was content to let the monotonous pounding from the boom box and the effect of the trading-post liquor lift the tin shed off that bare lot to a station far off in space.

Luis plunked down the bottle, sealing a decision. He groped deep in a pocket of his baggy pants and came up with a clamshell cell identical to one I'd seen before.

"Is a camera phone," he said, opening it, "same kind as Juanito's, so I can send him pictures and he can send me."

My face felt hot. The *bump-bump* from behind the bar throbbed in the nerve ends. It was a clammy autumn night and the place was unheated, but it was as if someone had opened a furnace door in front of me. I'd turned in my chair to take my shadow off what he was getting ready to show me, but it had its own source of light. That's where the heat was coming from.

PART THREE

HIGH HORSE

EIGHTEEN

Sometimes I feel like I'm my own grandfather.

I'm old enough to remember when picture-taking was a big deal. The rest of the family got dressed up and gathered before the mother, who held a black box at her waist and gazed down interminably through the top-mounted viewfinder to get the composition Just Right while the smiles of her subjects set into concrete. Fifty years before that, a professional hunkered under a black cloth behind an instrument the size of an ammunition crate, squeezed a bulb, and ignited a hodful of magnesium in a blinding white flare. His predecessors packed mules up mountains and down canyons with a bigger box yet and a trunk filled with developing chemicals and glass plates, and used head braces to hold their parlor subjects still during an exposure that required sixty seconds without stirring to ensure a clear, grimly unsmiling image.

Now I sat in a tin can full of smoke and rancid music looking at a photo the size of a Christmas seal, captured with the twitch of a thumb and gathered from pixels that could put a man behind bars for the rest of his life.

Luis held the camera phone angled away from the nearest table of drinkers and just out of my reach in case I tried to lunge for it, but even at that distance the picture was sharp enough to identify the man in it if I ever saw him; and I was sure I would. He was a stranger to me, sheathed in a gray turtleneck and what appeared to be tight chinos, but that would be made of Lycra or spandex to give full range to his muscles and joints. At a glance, he appeared to be dancing, balanced delicately on the ball of one foot while raising the other to show the neoprene sole of a flexible shoe aimed straight for the camera. A narrow, youthful face that appeared to be at least part Asian twisted in a grimace, not of pain but of deep focus, with the lips curled back from the teeth in a tiger's snarl.

It was a riveting shot, and the last thing Johnny Toledo had ever seen.

There were details enough in the background to place the location as inside Johnny's squatter's haven on the Northwest side. Even the golden cherub he'd set so much store by was visible, teetering on its folding TV tray an instant before it toppled off.

I sat back, fumbling out a cigarette and trying to get it going without looking as if it was the first one I'd ever smoked. "I saw something like that in a book once. A photographer in Africa snapped a lion, just before it snapped him."

"Is not Africa." Luis flipped the phone shut.

"Know him?"

He shook his head. "Never seen him around, neither."

"He's built like you, probably not much older. Could he be running with a gang?"

"Gangs I know don't take yellows."

I got my wallet back out and palmed some bills. "Ask you something?"

He shrugged again. There was a whole conversation there.

"How do you reconcile selling cigarettes on the street with how your grandfather died?"

"Reconcile?"

"Justify. You know what I mean."

"I do not hold a gun to their head. No one held a gun to his."

"You've got a future as a spokesman for Big Tobacco. How much for the phone?"

He frowned. "Five hundred."

I snapped another hundred straight and slid it under the glass. His eyes followed it. Nothing else moved.

"Is three."

"What will you do with the money?"

"Put it with the rest until I am sixteen, then fly to Spain and run with the bulls."

I added two more bills to the pile. He had the reflexes of a rabbit. I pinned his wrist to the bench with my hand just as he fisted them and leaned his weight forward to make a dash for the door. The bottle of Bushmill's wobbled on its base like a tenpin. I caught it with my other hand just before it fell. The movement turned two heads at the nearest table, but only for a second.

Luis' eyebrows shot high. "If you move so fast yesterday, we would talk this talk then."

I let go of the bottle and held out my palm. He moved his shoulder once again and slapped the cell onto it. I let go of his wrist. The five hundred disappeared into the red jacket.

"Mexico's closer and cheaper," I said. "You can run with the bulls there, and you don't have to wait till you're sixteen. Go now."

He was standing. He lifted his chin. "I am not a cripple."

I held up the phone. "He'll take care of that, then finish the job after you've told him where this is."

His grin was almost as bright as the camera screen; it lit up that gloomy corner. "I send you a postcard from Mexico City."

After he left I weighed the cell on my palm. Balance weights shifted in my head, assuming a pattern based on that Asian face. It tripped something in my memory I'd thought was dead, or obsolete at the worst. I got up, put the phone in my pocket, and picked up the Irish for the cab driver. Half the world was Asian. It didn't have to mean anything. Most things don't. But I was grateful for the German engineering in the small of my back.

NINETEEN

The building was a quiet single story of new-looking red brick at the corner of Grand River and Schaefer. A Tigers pitcher could stand on the roof of my building and hit it with a fastball, if the team had a bull pen. It wasn't as new as it looked; sandblasting had ground decades of auto exhaust and pigeon incontinence off the bricks and glaziers had replaced the discolored windowpanes with bulletproof glass. In the old days it had been the second police precinct. Now it's Detroit Homicide.

It lacked the charms of 1300 Beaubien, with its tall arched windows and interior of marble and mahogany and brass; but also its rotten floors and weeping ceilings, mementoes of generations of looters in the office of mayor. Once you got past the metal detector, the new place looked like the accounting department of any modern corporation, illuminated from behind frosted glass panels and alive with the twee noises made by desktop computers and printers. On my way to the heart of the order I overheard more telephone conversations in cubicles about ethanol futures than prior arrests.

John Alderdyce's name was lettered in platinum on more frosted glass. When he barked and I opened the door, I might have been in one of those movies where an actor turns a knob on location in Delaware and steps into a studio interior in Southern California. The room looked as if it had been lifted by a crane from its original upper floor downtown and lowered onto this spot. The big plane table he used for a desk was the same and what looked to be the same stacks of file folders and jackets bound with giant rubber bands covered it in seeming disarray; in fact they were arranged according to a personal filing system that was harder to figure out than Stonehenge. Alderdyce's police academy class picture hung on the same nail at the same drunken angle, the same scanner bound with friction tape to protect it when it fell spat and crackled on top of a pile of blank forms, and the same face made up of dark matter watched me from behind the desk. The gravitational pull the inspector exerted on every free-floating object that drifted into his orbit hadn't lost its strength with the move; if anything it was even more powerful at ground level.

The academy picture had a rusty sepia look, the young faces shaved and shorn at the temples like members of an old-time baseball team, depressingly turn-of-the-twentieth century. He'd graduated only a class ahead of me.

"I've cracked more half-baked alibis with that picture than a team of men with rubber hoses," he said, tracking the line of my vision. "They can't sit still for wanting to get up and put it straight, especially the ex-cons. The correctional officers in this state make them be orderly."

"My old partner said the North Koreans used to booby-trap crooked pictures to blow up when GI's tried to straighten them."

"They won't let us have explosives. You missed the grand opening, if that's why you're here. The bottled water flowed like champagne."

It was morning. I'd taken a taxi to OK Towing & Repair, collected my Cutlass and what was left of my suit coat from what was left of the Plymouth Gran Sport, parked in the usual lot down from my building, and walked the rest of the way. I'd determined to replace pills with exercise. Now I sat in the folding metal chair facing the desk and crossed my legs, tugging at the knee of my trousers to disguise the spasms in the long muscle of the game one. I slipped the clamshell phone from the inside breast pocket of my sport coat and balanced it atop one of his stacks.

He left it there. "I've got one, too. I miss cranking for the operator."

"It isn't mine."

"Lost and Found's at Thirteen Hundred."

"You didn't find one at Johnny Toledo's, did you?"

His expression didn't change, but it meant nothing. When it did it was strictly a hydraulic operation. "All we found was Johnny, all broken up into puzzle pieces. The coroner's busy putting them together to see what's missing. No big stash of cash in the place either, so there's one more urban legend laid to rest. Where'd you get it?"

"You didn't ask if it's Johnny's."

"Sometimes I ask them out of order."

"Sometimes I answer them the same way," I said. "It's Johnny's, but it's not the one he carried. He bought a pair and gave one to a kid who ran errands for him."

"Who's the kid?"

"His name's Luis. His grandfather was the greatest bull-fighter in the history of Argentina."

"Whose wasn't? Where's he hang out?"

"Mexico, if he's as smart as he is fast." I gave it to him then, from the foot chase I'd left out before to last night's exchange in the blind pig. I didn't tell him the rest of Luis' name. He'd need the head start in case he hadn't jumped on my advice right away.

"We'd've closed the Marcus Garvey years ago if it wasn't the best place to start looking for all the landed scum in town." So far he hadn't touched the cell. It might not have been there at all. "What you're telling me is when Johnny's phone didn't turn up by his body you figured the killer kiped it, in case he got a message off to this Luis, who gave you a nice run through some of our more colorful neighborhoods."

"I almost had him the second time, until he ran down a one-way street."

"Ah. Shame on you. You made that haircut story so convincing I was going to ask you to recommend the barber."

"I am ashamed. I don't enjoy taking advantage of your native gullibility."

"What'd he tell Luis over the cell?"

"Nothing. It was while he was being stomped on and he wouldn't have had the time or breath."

He watched me, his eyes burning steady as filaments under the ledge of his brow. "If an upgrade's all you wanted, you can do a hell of a lot better for less than five hundred bucks."

"I doubt it. This one has a camera."

That took less than a second to sink in. He snatched it up and slung it open.

"That doohickey on the bottom, with a picture of an old-fashioned shutter job on it," I said.

"Shut the fuck up." He thumbed the button.

The skin tightened across his forehead as the image came up. It had been a long way from loose before. He'd lost flesh from age and the weight of the world, pasting skin to bone like shrink-wrap. His boys were grown and married, one of them was still speaking to him, and his wife, who earned more money than he did working shorter hours, was often away on business. Home for him was just a place to change horses between shifts.

None of this had come from him, although we'd known each other since we were children. The police community in Detroit is growing smaller along with the population, and no one in it has many secrets from the rest. Even a moth fluttering around its edges picks up morsels.

"This could be anything," he said finally.

"It could be. It isn't."

"He could be dancing."

"That cupid thing falling off the table behind him belonged to Johnny's old man, by right of theft. He kept it as a family heirloom. It didn't have a scratch on it until I found it yesterday, before I found Johnny. That fall put a big dent in it. I'll bet you the five hundred I gave Luis that when you blow up the picture there won't be a dent. That puts the time of the dance even with time of death."

"We don't know that's when it fell."

"Sure we do. You do and I do, and so does Luis."

"If we had his testimony, we could bracket the time between his visits: Johnny alive, Johnny dead, with this character filling the gap. Only we don't, so we can't. You went home to catch some winks and he hitched a ride to Mexico."

"He's got a better chance of staying alive there than in an eight-by-ten room in County." I tapped a finger on his desk. "Double or nothing says something else shows up when you blow it up. Blood."

"Ketchup from one of Johnny's hot dogs. You can't do a chemical analysis on a photographic image."

"You can't convict anyone at all if you don't pick him up. This is way better than a police sketch. How many Asian whirligigs are in town this season?"

"One less than usual, probably. Assassins don't hang around once they're made."

"This one took Johnny's cell. That means he knows what's on it and where he sent it. He'll hang around long enough to make the set complete."

He transferred a stack of sheets from a telephone console, lifted the receiver, and tapped a key. "Hornet." He cradled the receiver without waiting for an answer.

The lieutenant opened the door ten seconds later, filling the frame. He scowled when he saw me. "Holding or County?" he asked Alderdyce.

"Walker's not under arrest. Run this down to the photo lab and tell them to get prints of the picture on it." He stuck out the cell.

Hornet balanced it on his palm like a compass. "That's an errand for a uniform."

"I'd run it down myself if I didn't have more to talk about with Walker. The fewer hands it passes through, the less chance some fumblefuck has to delete what's on it by accident."

"What is it?"

"A possible inspectorship for you. Retirement for me with the rank of commander."

He seemed to draw a conclusion close to correct. His thought processes worked just fine or the department would have turned him out years ago as a health risk. "Want me to call Marshal Thaler?"

"Let's keep it local for now."

"Yessir, Inspector." He took his baggy grin out with the phone.

Alderdyce measured the height of my eyebrows. They were up around my hairline. "It'd mean another meeting, and nothing ever gets done in those. It's bad enough I've got to share this one with those assholes in Narcotics. Drugs are just a gimmick in the case. When a mistake gets made and someone sends out a life-taker to tidy up, it's Homicide. I can't work where I can't swing my elbows without poking someone on either side."

"How sure are we it was a mistake?"

"Dumping a load of grade-five heroin where there isn't a user in a carload who can afford crack without making a withdrawal from some party store? Even Santa Claus does better market research than that."

"Who says money's the motive?"

"I thought about that for about half a second," he said. "I'm a detective. Nut-job killers and terrorists bitch up the whole process of investigation. It's tough enough to make a case for means, motive, and opportunity if the motive is you're just mad at someone else or you want to scare the shit out of a lot of people you've never met."

"It doesn't have to be that kind of terrorism. Maybe some-one's just mad at Detroit, or using Detroit as a test lab for something bigger. They say Baby Face Nelson used to throw cops off his tail by dumping cash out his car window. Unload-ing industrial-strength dope by the long ton packs an even big-ger punch: an OD on every block."

He chuckled deep in his chest, like corn popping in a cave. "Find a part for Godzilla and you can sell that one to Holly-wood. Just now I'm going to concentrate on picking up our dancer."

"Is it all right if I go on looking for those converter boxes? This is the last day I owe Crossgrain."

"I'd almost forgotten about those. Just don't turn the wrong way down any more one-way streets."

"I'm driving my own car now. The tail you're pinning on me will want to know that."

"Hornet told you that wasn't us before. He's a fat lazy slob who chews with his mouth open, but he's no liar."

"I've seen him eat. I'd rather he lied. I just thought it was the city's turn."

"Manpower's at rock bottom. We're sweeping up every pusher in town and turning 'em heels up to shake loose some of that primo horse. There's just no room left in the budget for a loose pin like you. We can always trail you later by the litter you leave behind." He flipped open a folder and started reading.

I got up. At the door I said, "Give any thought to what happens when that heroin supply stops?"

"Only every waking minute."

A sergeant with the stoic gaze and sharp beak of a snapping turtle watched me from his station as I made for the exit with my phone ringing, a generic tone that had come with the package; I'd left a far more sophisticated piece of portable technology with the department. He returned his attention to his entry log as I pushed through the heavy glass door, fumbling in my pocket.

"Mr. Walker, this is Eugenia Pappas. May I see you right away?"

There were no ambient noises on her end, not even air stirring in the large room where she'd be bottled up like the authentic imported her late husband's father had reserved for magistrates and better. She herself might have been ordering office supplies; but that wasn't her job.

"Is it about Ouida?"

"In person, please. I want to retain your professional services."

I told her I was on my way. The season was picking up.

TWENTY

Halloween is good for Detroit, once you overlook that business about widespread arson on Devil's Night.

The DPW sells special trash bags to civic-minded homeowners that when they're filled and placed at the curb make giant orange jack-o'-lanterns. Genuine pumpkins with grins carved in them flicker on front porches, ghosts made from bed linens and papier-mâché flutter from the carcasses of trees blasted by emerald ash disease, and shops specializing in costumes and decorations string bright temporary banners across empty storefronts where retailers bent on permanence have failed. With the surviving trees in full color, it looks like a living city.

Beyond the limits the leaves turned sodden, hanging like spit curls from glistening branches and pasting themselves so tight to the windshield the wipers slid over them without disturbing them, like a wallpaper brush. The spattery rain we'd had earlier had gathered force as it swept toward Canada, drumming the vinyl roof of the Cutlass and racing along the gutters. Out on St. Clair the lancets stitched up the surface and the low clouds turned the water the color of tarnished silver. A bicyclist made a picture of misery sawing at his pedals on a sidewalk paved treacherously with slick foliage, his athletic shoes squishing on each turn. I powered down to crawl through a puddle the size of a lagoon to avoid splashing him.

Under those conditions the cockeyed Bauhaus architecture of the Pappas house made sense, its uneven roofline leaning like so many sails into the slanting rain. The miniature Greek flag on the mailbox that matched the house jiggled before the wind circling back off the bay.

I turned up the collar of the sport coat and ran for the covered porch, but I got a good dose just the same. I stood in a puddle and used the Zeus-head knocker. I half expected Ouida to answer in her suit and cranberry hair, but the other half suspected why I'd been summoned. I wasn't surprised when Eugenia Pappas opened the door.

"You're soaked."

"It sounded urgent, so I swam over. She still missing?"

She told me to come in. I closed the door behind me and wiped my feet on a coconut mat. She looked less angular standing than she had all coiled up at her desk, tall and strong-boned in a lightweight wool dress a shade off from the one she'd had on before, her long, blue-veined feet stuck in slippers with low heels. The silver inlay in her pale, pulled-back hair glinted like platinum wire in the light reflecting off the porcelain bric-a-brac in the foyer. When she seemed satisfied I wouldn't leave wet tracks on the floor, she turned and led me into the morning room.

The curtains were drawn back today, providing a wide-angle view of the bay glowering under the overcast. The rain appeared to have settled into one spot, turning the water to hammered tin. The level seemed to be rising as I was looking at it.

"When I still hadn't heard from her this morning, I sent someone around to her apartment. He talked the manager into letting him in with a passkey. He found the place orderly, the bed a little messed up the way she might have left it when she came to work yesterday morning. Nothing in her papers or on her answering machine to indicate where she'd gone or why. While he was looking around, this call came in here." She pressed a button on a small telephone counsel balanced on the corner of the Prairie desk.

A metallic-sounding voice issued from the speaker, each word dropping with equal emphasis, sounding as human as marbles falling into a bowl: "We . . . have . . . Ouida. Wait . . . for . . . our . . . call."

"I'm not in the habit of answering the phone myself," she said when the message clicked off. "When Ouida isn't here, I let the machine get it."

"You were expecting your man to report from her apartment."

"I know Ouida's number, and the number of his cell. The ID was blocked. How is that possible?"

"Star sixty-seven. It isn't a state secret. No use asking if you recognized the voice. It could be a man's or a woman's scrambled, or computer-generated. Are you still waiting for the call?"

She shook her head. "I turned on the machine when it came in thirty minutes ago." She pushed the button again. The same mechanical arrangement of syllables directed her to deliver the entire shipment of TV converter boxes she'd received to the corner of Michigan and Trumbull in Detroit. She'd tried to ask questions in a voice strung tight, but the directions continued without interruption. The time of the appointment was an hour past dark that evening. A click and a dial tone cut her off in the middle of another question.

"You were talking to a recording," I said. "Do they have her, do you think?"

"I have to assume they do. She wouldn't have stayed away this long without word if something hadn't happened."

"Do you have the boxes?"

"I don't, honestly. That I know of." She stroked a bony upper arm abstractedly. "It's possible Ouida tracked them down and didn't have the chance to tell me. If she did and they're in my possession, they could be in any one of a dozen places: storage sheds, warehouses, the homes of volunteers and people I employ. My charitable work involves auctions of donated goods, recycled clothing and furniture, bottled water and blankets and other emergency supplies for families forced out of their homes by fire. The merchandise is spread out across three counties. Some of the volunteers are recovering addicts, people on parole, former homeless. Their inventory skills are rudimentary, to put it kindly. I've placed some calls, but it will be a miracle if we find those boxes before tonight. If they exist."

"The information might be in Ouida's computer."

"I know next to nothing about them. Do you?"

"No, but I know someone who does." I asked to use her telephone. She handed me the receiver and I pecked out Barry Stackpole's number. "They didn't say it has to be you making the delivery," I said as I waited for him to pick up. "You don't want to be in that neighborhood after dark. Not since they built Comerica Park. You know what's at Michigan and Trumbull?"

"I'm afraid I know little more about Detroit than I do about computers. I'm from Philadelphia originally. The stories Nick told me about what went on down there frightened me away from ever visiting the place."

"It's old Tigers Stadium. Anything can happen in a big empty shell like that. It might as well happen to me as anyone. Barry? Amos Walker."

The voice on the other end wouldn't have been out of place on prom night. "What are you doing calling from Nick Pappas' old number?"

"I see you upgraded your photographic memory to digital." I gave him a thumbnail of the situation. "Think you can lift what we need off the P.C. she left behind?"

"Depends on the incentive."

I put a hand over the mouthpiece. "Seven-fifty, to start. That covers expenses."

"Agreed," she said.

"You're on the sheet," I told Barry.

"Put it toward a correspondence course on DNA. I want a seat on Eugenia Pappas' board of directors. Tell her I'm feeling charitable."

"Who is this man?" she said when I'd delivered the message.

"He's an investigative journalist, specializing in organized crime."

"Don't you know anyone else who's good with technology?"

"A few, but I trust Barry."

"Let me speak to him, please."

I gave her the receiver and went over to the window to watch the rain skidding off the opposite side of the lake. The clouds had lifted slightly, letting sunlight slide under it, an eerie sight. The choppy surface appeared to be artifically lit, like a studio exterior in an old Technicolor movie. I turned back when she hung up.

"Obstinate man. We reached a compromise. No seat on the board of any of my foundations, but an unpaid press agent's position. It will give him a chance to check the veracity of our press releases before they reach the public."

"Dangerous concession on your part."

"Not at all. After Nick died I ran all the rats out of the base- ment. If there's anything unlawful going on in my operation, I want to know about it first. That was *his* concession."

"Ouida told me she'd report to you before she told me any- thing. You run a tight ship."

She smiled, a tight-lipped V in her angular face. "I paid attention when my husband spoke. His Old Country ances- tors were fishermen, and his father and grandfather piloted boatloads of contraband across the Detroit River." She nod- ded. "I run a tight ship."

I made a decision that was bound to get me in trouble. "This kind of contraband is worse than radio tubes and cases of Old Log Cabin, Mrs. Pappas. Those boxes are dummies filled with heroin."

"Why are you telling me this?" she said after a moment.

"I'm under what amounts to a federal gag order not to, so I hope you're as straight as you make out. People in the drug trade are a lot quicker on the trigger than most smugglers, and the people behind this deal make the regulars look like Muppets. You and Ouida seem close."

"If I'd thought a daughter of mine would turn out like her, I wouldn't have avoided pregnancy all those years."

"You need to be prepared for the fact that she may already be dead. This outfit is conscientious about cleaning up after itself. Two people are dead as a direct result, and the stuff they allowed to leak out through those boxes has been killing habitual users all across town for a week. I want your permission to bring in the authorities."

"You certainly cannot have it. You heard the instructions: no police, no FBI, no one in law enforcement. One lone courier or they'll kill Ouida. I hear what you're saying, but I can't take the chance if there's any possibility at all she's still alive. I literally could not live with myself if she were to die because of something I did."

I started to say something, but she went on. "I know you're skeptical when I say I've separated myself entirely from my past with Nick. I wasn't a barefoot, ignorant wife; I knew the kind of business he was in even if I didn't know all the details. I know some people died in its pursuit, and I know he was directly responsible in at least two cases. The detectives who came to interview him didn't know that.

"I'm getting to be an old woman. The immaterial things mean more to me now. Frankly, I'm frightened of what awaits me. I intend to buy salvation the same way Nick bought himself and his people out of trouble with the courts."

"There's an inherant weakness in that line of thought, if you're a Christian."

"I'm not sure I am, although I've donated fortunes to the Greek Orthodox Church. All my sins postdate Christ, so I don't accept that He died for them. But Christianity doesn't hold the monopoly on the afterlife. You can call my plan a cynic's perversion of faith, but I'm a practical devout. I'm very fond of Ouida. I like to think I'd do anything in my power and beyond it to bring her back safe strictly out of the kindness of my heart, but if I'm the cause of her death, it means everything I've invested in my spiritual delivery up to this point will come to nothing. I can't write it off, and I can't afford to die in a state of celestial bankruptcy."

"You will, though, regardless. You can't buy holy indulgence. The bottom fell out of that market when the Spanish Inquisition went bust."

"It's enough that you know where I stand. If you go against my wishes in this matter and the worst happens, I'll have nothing to lose. But you will. You and your friend Barry Stackpole."

"That speech usually comes with a gun in someone's hand."

"I held one only once, when it was given to me as a gift. But I know how to dial a telephone."

I pinched a cigarette from the pack and rolled it along my lower lip. Her nostrils turned white; plainly it was a nonsmoking house. I said, "And you've separated yourself from Nick how?"

TWENTY-ONE

Barry showed up looking like a cable installer. I might not have recognized him coming up the driveway if it weren't for the rolling sailor's walk he'd developed to throw off muggers who specialized in cripples. He'd slid his athletic frame into plain dark blue coveralls, slanted a cap to match over his right eyebrow, and carried a black metal toolbox the size of a dwarf's coffin. His face was the same vintage as mine, but he ironed his more often and packed it in ice overnight. It belonged on the cover of an Archie comic book.

I let him in and introduced him to Eugenia Pappas. There was a little hesitation before they shook hands. "I know you now," she said. "There was a bombing incident."

He met her reserved smile with a broad one of his own. They were equally synthetic. There was no sign in hers of the incipient madness she'd shown only twenty minutes earlier, and none in his to indicate how he felt about anyone connected with organized crime. "It's only an incident when it happens to someone else. Where's the box?"

"The box? Oh, the computer. I'll take you to it."

Ouida's office was across from the morning room, a square space done in cocoa brown and cool pinks with a window looking north. On the lawn a woman carved from chalky limestone stood pouring water from a jar into a basin at her feet, her drapery gathered down around her hips. Beyond that a line of blue spruce discouraged surveillance from the neighbors.

"Impressive," said Barry. "Nick hired a landscape architect to inconvenience the FBI without turning the place into a prison. You've done a nice job of keeping it up."

"The FBI lost interest many years ago. I maintain the screen for privacy, not security." Mrs. Pappas sounded patient.

"Yeah. Funny how the money turns clean after it circulates a couple of hundred times, just like the water gushing out of that naked lady's jug." He set down his toolbox, spun his cap backward, and straddled the chair facing the computer desk. The screen saver on the slim monitor was a montage of sepia images including the Eiffel Tower, the Arc de Triomphe, and a Frenchified Victorian portrait of a woman with pixiesh features and frank eyes. I didn't know Ouida's literary namesake from crêpes suzette, but anyone can guess.

We watched Barry play riffs on the keyboard until a password was called for. "No hunches?"

Eugenia said no. "I had to learn a whole new language when Nick died, or be taken to the cleaner's. It exhausted my capacity. When I couldn't afford to ignore the new technology any longer, I hired someone I could trust. It would defeat the purpose if I stood looking over her shoulder all the time."

"Trust and sex drive the economy. Otherwise, the same old money would keep passing through the same old hands until it wore clean out." He leaned down, opened the toolbox, rummaged in a compartment, and came up with something that looked like a Pez dispenser, which he inserted in a portal in the side of the computer tower. Something shuddered, the screen changed, and combinations of numbers and letters piled up in rows, filling the monitor from left to right and top to bottom. The image scrolled upward to make room for more. Barry sat back, unconsciously flicking the two empty fingers of the flesh-colored glove on his injured hand against the edge of the keyboard.

"Little invention of my own, with some technical assistance from a hacker I helped spring from Jackson," he said. "Programming it to run every possible combination of characters was the easy part. The hard part was coming up with a cookie to fool the computer into thinking each attempt was the first. Most security programs shut down after two or three failures."

I asked how long it usually took.

"Two hours is the record. It can take days."

Eugenia said, "We don't have days."

"You can pare the odds by calling your people. Maybe you'll get lucky and turn those converters before Black Bart here warms up."

"The western stagecoach bandit?" I asked.

"No, the eighteenth-century pirate. Bartholomew Roberts took four hundred ships, a hundred times as many as that blowhard Blackbeard, and still the mark to beat. No one else came close, even in Hollywood."

"I'll make those calls," Eugenia said. "This is making me a nervous wreck."

Barry waited a few seconds after the door shut, to give her

time to lose patience listening at the keyhole. "She as nuts as they say?"

"I haven't heard what they say."

"The local Greek Orthodox church declined a generous offer to endow a youth recreation center when she wouldn't budge on drawing a halo around Nick's head on the plaque."

"Nuttier. She thinks Saint Peter's a headwaiter: table for one with a view of Eden on a twenty-buck tip."

"Who's to say she's wrong? What makes Paradise different from an evening at the Rooster Tail?"

"That's blasphemous even for you."

"I sold my soul to Scratch when I joined the Press Club. What's important about those converters?"

I hesitated. "You can't use it."

"For how long?"

"Forever, at a conservative estimate. I'd like not to be the first private cop hanged for treason."

"Ah. The spooks. Mob Lite. You lack the soul of a pioneer. Shoot the works."

I did. There was no use holding back from him. What you didn't give him he went out and got.

He said, "I heard about Johnny. Rotten shame. If it wasn't for enterprising types like him, we'd be up to our eyes in junk cars and refrigerators. Those scraphounds have done more for recycling than Greenpeace and the EPA combined. I'd push for a statue if I thought it would stand two hours before one of Johnny's competitors got to it. They snatched four bronze Titans from a civic center last year. That takes a crane and two flatbed trailers."

"Even Greenpeace doesn't recycle material currently in use by its legal owners."

"Give 'em time. No mention of converter boxes in the Toledo kill: cagy, those counterintelligence wonks. I flagged that Crossgrain case, and I've been tracking these heroin O.D.s for old times' sake, but I didn't make a connection."

"Somebody screwed up major league. The stuff's white as cotton. You don't throw it away on a place like Detroit."

"Not unless you're running a field test."

"I thought of that. They don't need guinea pigs. An operation this well-heeled, with sources in the Golden Triangle, has all it needs to measure quality in a controlled environment, without the risk of attracting attention from the authorities."

"An operation with those connections is its own authority. But I'm not talking quality. I mean witnessing the effects in actual practice. What if nobody screwed up at all? What if high-test dope is this year's hijacked passenger plane and someone wanted to see how well it worked, in a place the rest of the country's already given up on so nobody'd notice?"

"New Orleans'd be a better bet."

"Too much press since Katrina. Bunch of dead junkies in the Motor City? Let's see what's on Channel Six."

"I bounced the terrorist angle off John Alderdyce," I said. "He shot it down."

"Once he gets his teeth in, he wouldn't give up jurisdiction if Osama turned up in a sweep. Also he may be thinking of the wrong kind of terrorist. You said this killer Johnny took the picture of is Asian?"

"They recruit Asians."

"So does China, and exclusively."

"China's not a terrorist nation."

"It's worse. It's a communist country breaking out in a

severe case of capitalism. Mao and the little Maos that followed him spent fifty bloody years wiping out the tongs, but now that the economy's off the waterwheel standard, it's opened itself back up to all the benefits and disadvantages of free enterprise, including organized crime. Same thing happened in Japan after V-J Day and in Russia after the Iron Curtain fell. Heard of the Chih Kou?" He spelled it in Roman letters, but it sounded like *Sure Cow*.

"I'm guessing it isn't a cocky Hereford."

"It means Paper Dog. It's the most populous of the societies that manage smuggling, gambling, and extortion in the People's Republic. That's old information. NATO and the CIA have been sniffing around after tips that the Paper Dog is dividing its various interests into subsocieties, each specializing in a single area of crime. Naturally, the Dog has rivals: Tears of the Dragon, White Silk Pig, half a dozen others that also sound like rock bands. There have been street shootings, storefronts bombed, a prominent importer-exporter with ties to the Dog sliced into pieces and divvied up in empty lots and alleys from Chungking to Shanghai."

"Sounds like Chicago 1929."

"More like Manchuria 1922. Some of the leaders claim direct descent from the warlords of that period; they host long, elaborate feasts wearing ceremonial masks and bamboo armor. They say at one of them a suspected informant was fed to a crocodile. That may be an urban legend. I'd give plenty to be Chinese and crash one of those dinners."

He wasn't being facetious. He had a Pulitzer Prize and his name in the acknowledgments of hundreds of books about hoodlums, but for him the real attraction of investigative journalism was the opportunity to play dress-up. The FBI had four files of telephoto shots of thugs it hadn't identified, all of them Barry under the sharkskin suits, wigs, and false noses.

I shook my head. "I've got to start spending some quality time with CNN. This is all news to me."

"It still would be if you did. Apart from the fact that Anchor Ken and Stand-up Barbie are too busy diving in celebrity Dumpsters to cover it, the government in Beijing is just as repressive as it always was. The Chinese press won't report any story that casts a negative light on its so-called liberalization, and the investigation by Western agencies is top secret. Officially, the population there is happy with its Lee Riders and Stones tickets. Hatchetmen are ancient imperial history."

I didn't bother asking how Barry knew different. He was on the receiving end of an Internet the Internet itself knew nothing about. "This is all starting to sound just a little bit Sax Rohmer."

"Those old-time pulp writers never got the recognition they deserved. Criminal mastermind plotting to overthrow the West by way of a shadowy underground organization spread across the globe? What was the old boy smoking in that pipe of his?"

"So who's the mastermind?"

"No clue so far. That's his name for now: No Klu So Fa. This notion of the modern underworld being run by a board of directors is a smoke screen to discourage personal advancement through assassination. There's always someone up top giving the orders. Conventional intelligence is No Klu So Fa encourages these clowns to parade around in costume to draw lightning away from him. That plan has worked up till now, but one of these days he'll be forced to show himself. You have to lead a movement to go forward. You can't push it from behind." He was monitoring the rows of characters racing across the screen out of the corner of one eye. "One of these subsocieties I mentioned specializes in training professional assassins. It's got its own compound somewhere in Manchuria, complete with mockup city streets for acting out real-life scenarios, just like at Quantico."

I saw where he was headed. "We don't know for sure our guy's Chinese. The picture was too small to make out details."

"Even a cheap digital blows up sharper than most film. I wish you'd come to me with it before you went running to the cops."

"Yeah. Did I mention they hang you for treason?"

"They use lethal injection, which as we know now is neither cruel nor unusual. I understand it tickles. If the Dog is exporting talent, it could be a real break in smashing up these gangs before they get a foothold here."

"Can we save the Union tomorrow? Today I want to find Ouida."

"Would you settle for now for finding those converter boxes?"

I looked at the screen. It had changed while I was talking, swinging open like Ali Baba's door.

TWENTY-TWO

This can't be right."

Eugenia Pappas leaned back from her blanched pine desk, looking at the printout. Barry had accompanied me to the morning room, the features of which seemed to interest him more than the view of Anchor Bay, glittering under the sun breaking through the clouds. Bright-colored sails had sprung up like crocuses on the surface. The days to play with outdoor toys were growing short.

He said, "Ouida bookmarked it: ten boxes logged in yesterday morning. That's the day she went to lunch and never came back. Someone hacked into your system, knew about the shipment the same time she did."

"I mean the location. That warehouse has been empty for months. I'm negotiating with developers who want to raze it and build condos."

"It wouldn't be the first time someone used the Detroit riverfront to store contraband," I said. "How often do you take inventory?"

"Never. I employ people who do that."

"Shame on you," said Barry. "Nick knew every stolen tape deck in his possession and where to lay hands on it. In his racket he had to micromanage in order to keep the help from stealing him blind. It isn't like he taught them honesty by example."

"I resent that. You're in Nick's home."

I stepped in before the sparring started. "I believe you, Mrs. Pappas, so far as not dealing in dope. The work's dangerous enough for people with experience. If you've got an employee who's gone into business for himself, his reporting those boxes would give him the chance to pass the buck to the top in case the cops got nosy. He might have accepted that shipment before Crossgrain's murder was reported. A garden-variety burglary wouldn't have rated high enough for you to be asked to check the books. He might have rung up the sale based on the going rate for converters and shipped the heroin profits off to Switzerland."

"But you asked me about the boxes before there was a murder."

"I'm not the police. It rated high enough with me. Your chiseler wouldn't know I'd been hired to find the boxes."

"I'll arrange to have them picked up." She scooped up her telephone.

Barry reached over and thumbed down the plunger. "We'll pick them up. All part of the service."

I said, "If you tip off the help, the snow will drift to another location. If we deliver ten empty boxes to the stadium, that's how many pieces you'll get Ouida back in."

She replaced the receiver, frowned, drew open a shallow drawer, and took out a checkbook bound in printed silk.

"This is more than I asked for," I said, when she'd handed

me the check she'd written. "Barry's here because of your agreement, not to split the bill."

"You can do what you like with the extra. The original amount was for risking your life to bring Ouida back. Now you're suggesting risking your life a second time just to obtain what the kidnappers are after. You might want to cash it before you set out. The beneficiary of your estate will never find a bank that will honor a check made out to a dead man."

"This *is* my estate." I put the check in my wallet. "Three times, by the way, not two."

"I'm sorry?"

"Risking my life. You promised to kill us both if we ring in the cops."

"You didn't tell me that part," Barry said. "You know, I canceled an interview with the governor for this."

"You're welcome."

Barry was driving a buzzy little sports job with an emerald finish and the top folded down. It would be a gift from some high-placed snitch in return for keeping their association a gentleman's affair, registered to some branch of some corporation whose comptroller didn't know his stock options depended on the house advantage in Las Vegas. The arrangement was a conflict of interest only if Barry put anything more into it than his customary silence. He disliked owning things outright. It made them harder to part with if he had to take off in the middle of some night. That long-ago bomb had taken away more than a leg and sundry other pieces of his body; it had blown apart his faith in the permanence of anything.

I followed him to the garage where he stored the car, just

down from the converted department store where he rented his apartment on a month-by-month basis, waited until he climbed in next to me, and let out the clutch while he transferred the big chrome fifty-caliber magnum from the slash pocket of his coveralls to the glove compartment.

"If you packed lighter, you wouldn't have to keep moving it around all the time," I said.

"It's no trouble."

"You don't have to do this. I brought you in for your computer skills."

"Wish I'd never developed them. I used to spend most of my time doing this. Pushing a mouse around a pad is not why I joined the Fourth Estate."

"Everything gets old, even riding with the U.S. Cavalry."

It was coming on noon. The business-lunch traffic was heading out of town to where the restaurants were. We turned off Jefferson and crunched to a stop on gravel alongside a strip of bleached asphalt ending in a guardrail. Beyond the rail rolled the river, the color of brushed aluminum under the sun filtering through a scrim of smut from both sides of the international border.

The warehouse district, which used to stretch from the old Stroh's brewery all the way down to Toledo, Ohio—mile after mile of brick and block storage space stacked to the roofs with steel coils and sacks of grain—hardly qualifies as a district any more. Developers are renovating or knocking down the century-old piles one by one, establishing condominiums and lofts available at tenement rates in order to lure young professionals away from the suburbs. The earth there is corrupt to its center, drenched with toxic waste leeched from car batteries in storage and rusted chemical tanks, but the city issues waivers on a fixed-price menu. Variances are easier to obtain than dog licenses.

Barry got out and stuck the big magnum through his slash pocket into some kind of holster under his coveralls. "I was born way too late. I should've been shooting rumrunners with a Speed Graphic. They tied up right there." He pointed to where the ground sloped down from the guardrail and slid under the river.

"One flash and you'd be doing the tommy gun dance." I checked the magazine in the Luger and poked it away under the tails of my sport coat.

The warehouse Eugenia Pappas had directed us to was a community affair, a series of leased spaces in a homely barn that looked as if someone had gone over every inch of its brick exterior with a blowtorch; fires had razed generations of wooden buildings that had stood on the spot. Most of the recent maintenance had gone into replacing broken window-panes. Whole sections were more masonite than glass, and BBs had punched holes in most of the rest. Roman numerals chiseled into a cream-colored cornerstone fixed 1903 as the end of unchecked conflagration. A brick loading dock faced the river, where yard engines had chugged along rails long since torn up and sold for scrap, towing stove parts and lumber from cargo ships anchored off the bank before the coming of the guardrail to prevent wayward drunks from pitching their cars into the river. An iron sliding door designed to open onto the dock was secured with a padlock and chain.

"We could shoot if off," Barry said.

"We could. Self-inflicted gunshot wounds don't interest me."

"How unromantic of you. Well, I left my battering ram in my other pants."

"Here's a thought." I knocked on the door with the meaty part of my fist.

Nothing answered but the wind off the water and the smell of carp. I tried again, then stepped back and kicked at the door, bonging it in its heavy frame.

Barry touched my arm.

I turned and watched a stoop-shouldered figure in a tattered brown Carhartt coat and baggy green work pants coming our way around the corner of the building with his fists stuck deep in his pockets. His chin was plastered to his chest, giving us a view of a head of feathery dirty-gray hair that looked as if it had never been trained, an ambulatory dandelion gone to seed. His steel-toed work boots made twin channels in the gravel, leaving the ground only when he skipped at every fourth shuffle, a hurrying gait in his set. He kept right on coming until the top of the loading dock came flush with his chest, then took his hands out of his pockets and rested them on the dock; twisted, gray-white roots, painful even to look at. He showed his face then, screwed up against the diffused sunlight. It was as brown and wrinkled as a roasted potato.

"Lock's there for a purpose." His speech was a shrill twang, packed in from some prairie state, Kansas or Nebraska; some flat place where it cracked like a .22 rifle.

"So's this." I got down on one knee and snapped open a folded sheet under his nose. "This is a bill of lading signed by Eugenia Pappas in receipt for merchandise you're holding."

He didn't take it. I doubted his fingers opened far enough. He worked his lips over the syllables. His eyesight seemed sound. The sheet was greenish and nearly transparent, torn from a pad bequeathed by Nick Pappas. The date blank followed *19–*. Eugenia had filled it out, substituting the new century with a mark through the old, and signed it in a hand as angular as the rest of her.

He lifted his head from the sheet. "She's off her rocker. This is the easiest caretaking job I ever had. Nobody tries to bust into a place that's empty."

"When's the last time you looked inside?"

"What for? I got me a little office in the side with an outside door. Sleep there sometimes on this little cot, chase away kids with air pistols. I tell you there's nothing there."

"Chase 'em away? I thought you invited them around for variety." Barry kicked at a squashed copper pellet that had bounced off brick.

The old man tugged aside the collar of his coat to show him an angry red welt on his neck. "Mister, they don't pay me enough."

"Let's take a look anyway," I said.

He gathered the bones of his shoulders into a steeple behind his head and let them drop, turned, and shuffled back the way he'd come, following the tracks he'd made in the gravel. No skipping now. We hopped down from the dock and followed.

"What do they do, back-order these guys from Dickens?" Barry murmured.

We went in through a brown steel fire door labeled KEEP OUT and waited in a small square architect's mistake of a room with an army cot and a gray steel desk while the caretaker shook loose a key on a ring and inserted it in a door on the other side. The desk was littered with jointed pieces of plastic, squashed tubes of paint and cement, and what looked like a replica of the *Mayflower,* as it would have appeared half finished in the shipmaker's yard in Southampton. The solitary life is stuffed with crosswords and paint-by-numbers sets.

A gust of decayed wood and mildew came out when he opened the door, shredding a webwork as intricate as the Hanging Gardens of Babylon. Barry and I exchanged a look; steers don't come any bummer.

The storage area was a vast square space going twenty feet in every direction, including up to the rafters, where dynasties of birds had built nests. Descendants of the early founders fluttered off their perches when the current of air reached them, making new deposits onto the chalky splatter below. The panes that lingered in the windows, dirty and discolored and nearly opaque, cast the huge room in eternal twilight. Our feet scraped the concrete slab, making echoes. My toe collided with the skeleton of a small animal laid out intact on its side, as if in state, and sent it sliding like a shuttle.

"See?" The old man's voice cracked triumphantly. "When a rat can't live off what's here, man, it's empty."

As if in confirmation, a blast of wind off the river shook the building, dislodging sawdust and old ash off a wooden framework weakened by the last fire. A termite's sneezing fit would save some developer the cost of demolition.

"What's that?" Barry pointed at an uneven shape, vaguely rectangular, covered by a stiff canvas tarpaulin in a far corner.

"Wood pallets. It don't pay to haul 'em out to the curb."

"Why cover wood pallets?" I asked.

"If I start to ask why, I'll end up asking why anybody pays me to look after a great big box of nothing. At my age you don't have to look far to get depressed."

I approached the tarp-covered shape, stooped to hook a

hand under the hem, and turned it back, taking a step away in case a rat hadn't gotten the message. Nothing came out, but a puff of gray dust rose from the top and settled back. It didn't seem nearly enough dust for as much time had passed since a forklift truck had disturbed any of the pallets.

Barry broke the silence. "Never fails. No one ever leaves a place as tidy as he found it."

The pallets lay end to end and stacked three deep, with square shipping cartons arranged on top in three uneven rows. Each was stamped with the same legend:

MACARTHUR INDUSTRIES

TWENTY-THREE

The caretaker scratched his chin with a gnarled knuckle. For him it was the equivalent of a backflip. I asked him if he was there all the time.

"They don't chain me to the wall. I go home nights."

"That cobweb we came through took time to build," Barry said. "They had to have come in through the bay door. That means a key to the padlock, or they cut it off and replaced it. One pretty much looks like all the rest."

I said, "They had a key. You might go to that much trouble to take something out and cover your tracks, but not to put something in. Who do you punch in with?" I asked the old man.

"Nobody. It's just me here, day after day. Every other Friday the mailman comes in with my paycheck, signed by Mrs. Pappas."

I took the check she'd given me out of my wallet and showed it to him. "That the signature?"

"Can't say. Can't make it out."

"Well, if you can make it out on your paycheck well enough to know it's Mrs. Pappas' name, that means it's different."

Barry smiled. "Ouida won't starve."

I put away the check and lifted a carton off the top of one stack. It was lighter than it looked. I put it down, got out my pocket knife, and slit the sealing tape on the flap. A shallow rectangle made of black plastic slid out of the packing material. I couldn't believe I'd never heard of converter boxes only a couple of days ago. I used the point of the blade to loosen the tiny brass screws on the back panel and removed it. I showed Barry the empty cavity.

"Couple of kilos short," he said. "Check the rest."

I didn't have to open any more cartons. They were all equally lightweight.

"Decoys?" he asked.

"Now, maybe. They didn't start out that way. No circuit boards or wires. They were never intended to be hooked up. Somebody beat us to them."

"So what now?"

"Same plan."

"What about what you said about delivering empty boxes?"

"The directions said only boxes. No mention of heroin." When he stared I said, "I'm open to alternatives."

No answer. I lifted three boxes in a stack. He lifted two and we finished packing the trunk of the Cutlass in two trips. We left the caretaker in the little office holding two pieces of plastic together waiting for the cement to dry. With his hands the *Mayflower* would take as long to complete as the original.

"You haven't told me when and where's the drop," said Barry as I turned the key in the ignition.

"Doesn't matter to you. They said only one."

"So I'll ride on the floor in the backseat."

"I might risk it if I weren't already trying to run a bluff."

"Well, take along your cell. If they don't take it off you I can trace the signal to your body."

"Don't tell anyone I gave my life for better TV reception."

"It makes as much sense as risking it for a woman you met only once."

"We didn't even get along very well. But I get paid to find things."

"Me, too. You wouldn't be trying to protect a gimp, would you?"

"I'm a gimp myself."

"That leg ought to have healed by now."

"Talk to the leg."

He leaned back in the seat and took something out of the slash pocket opposite the one where he carried his gun. It was a little yellow plastic pill box he opened with the snap of a thumbnail. I looked at the Vicodin inside. "You too?"

"Headaches." He touched the place where his skull was patched. "Take some for later while you're at it. I've got un-limited refills."

I thanked him, put some tablets in my shirt pocket, and crunched down two. Just knowing they were in my system took the edge off.

"You're in great shape to take on a kung fu killer," he said.

"I will be when the pills kick in."

"When you meet him, look at his eyebrows."

"Don't tell me they're lethal too."

"Paper Dog assassins shave vertical lines in their eye-brows: five in the right, four in the left." He stroked his own with a forefinger. "It's how they recognize each other, and they can grow them out when they're in hiding. It's a tribute to the Gang of Nine, captured and beheaded in Nanking in 1925. I told you they've got a hard-on for those old warlords."

"Why do I need to know this?"

"In case he leaves enough of you to provide a deathbed identification."

Continuing up Woodward I flipped open my cell one-handed, drew the antenna out with my teeth, and thumbed out the number of Felonious Monk, but I didn't hit SEND. I'd had my best luck with Gale Kreski, aka Bud Lite, dropping in on him without announcement, and anyway I had nothing better to do to burn daylight until I was expected at Tigers Stadium.

It was one of those gift days we sometimes get well into autumn, not precisely Indian summer because there's no frost preceding them, but balmy enough to consider taking the Jet Ski out one more time before breaking out the moth-balls, if you didn't mind a slight risk of frostbite. It's not un-usual to see the proud owner of a convertible tooling along with the top down and earmuffs on, or someone sunning him-self on a porch roof with goosebumps on his tan. The morn-ing's rain had only dusted that part of town, leaving behind wet patches in the shade of saloons built like Fort Knox and a peppery smell of ozone.

I parked around the corner, on the side where an apartment house had shared a common wall with the extinct hardware store before it had been eaten by a wrecking ball; halfway up the brick, an old connecting door opened onto a straight twenty-foot drop. Above the trade entrance, the delinquent primate on the sign swung its switchblade, either a broad visual pun or a

statement of the owner's contempt for the cluelessness of his
customers.

I found him at the counter, with a faded napless towel
spread out on top and a dismembered saxophone littering the
towel with valves and stops and cork-ringed components, including a gleaming brass bell that looked like an old-fashioned
ear trumpet when not connected with the rest. He was using
an oily blue rag to polish a piece the size and shape of a pulled
tooth.

"Takes me back to boot camp," I said. "Nighttime guerrilla
training."

"Let me guess. You had to disassemble and put back together a rifle blindfolded." The resonant voice was in control,
like a powerful engine at idle. He went on polishing without
looking up.

"No, a carburetor. I tested negative for mechanical apti-
tude, so they trained me for the motor pool. Then when I got
to Southeast Asia they chucked it. I never saw an undercar-
riage my whole tour. But I can change your oil if you want."

Today he had his hair tied up in a red bandanna, a piratic
effect, with the sleeves cut off a plain sweatshirt and the riot
of tattoos spilling up his arms and under the fabric. He set
aside the toothy fragment, picked up the mouthpiece, and
blew through it, making a razzy sound with the reed. It might
have been commentary.

"What's happening in Guam?"

"My lawyer got another postponement. Those Chamorro
bodyguards I told you about? One of 'em landed in jail for
possession for sale of hashish."

"Think he knows anything?"

"When they weren't on duty, they were bombed out of

their minds on pot in Winfield's garage. Secrets are the first thing to go in that situation. If somebody reached one of them, paid him to look out at the ocean or cap Winfield himself, he knows. It all depends on how scared he is of being convicted of the other thing." He shook his head. "Wish it was something more than hashish. In the protectorates, that's like Starbucks."

"How's your defense fund?"

"Just now it's a race between how long that bodyguard holds out and when it gurgles empty. My credit line kind of fell apart when they booked me for murder."

I took out Eugenia Pappas' check and spread it out on a clear space on the towel. "I can endorse this over to you right now, or go to my bank and bring you back the cash. Whatever's more convenient."

He glanced at the amount, removed the split reed from the mouthpiece, and dropped the reed in a wastebasket on his side. "Is it legal? Right now I can't get a parking ticket. They'll revoke my bail."

"It's legal. It's dangerous. Could be fatal."

"Mister, you know the life expectancy of a mainlander in jail in Guam?"

"One question. You struck a fighting pose the other day. Was that a bluff or what?"

"I trained in martial arts since I was fourteen. It's all in the third track on my album: 'Gale Force.' "

"Should be the title track. When you get clear of this, you ought to consider going by your real name. Bud Lite sounds like the opening act at Soaring Island Casino."

"Bud Lite was that fucking Winfield's brainstorm. He'd've starved if there weren't always new talent to screw over." He started putting the saxophone back together. "What's the competition?"

"Imported Chinese talent. Two dead, that we know of. He doesn't open for anyone."

TWENTY-FOUR

I was giving him the particulars when a customer came in and loitered in the guitar-string section. Vintage Alice Cooper was playing on the store's sound system. He timed his browsing until the song finished, then selected a package, paid for it, and left without a word. He wore black from neck to heels, dyed his hair too dark for his complexion, and applied mascara with a spray gun.

"Can't be the real deal," I said, when the door closed behind him. "This day of all days, the true Goths should dress up as insurance salesmen."

Kreski made a noise in his throat. "Today's Halloween. I forgot. It was my favorite day of the year until all this shit came down. Put on fangs and a cape and get all that darkness out of your system just in time for the holidays. I could rent a ninja outfit for tonight."

"Come as you are. If things go as planned all you'll need is a phone. Got a cell?"

"I held out long as I could, but I can't afford to miss a call from my lawyer."

"I'm going to hang on to mine as long as I can, keep the line open. You'll be outside. When you hear the word, call the cops."

"What's the word?"

I thought. "Bud Lite."

"That's two words. Hard to work them into the kind of conversation you'll be having."

"Not as hard as you think. It's Tigers Stadium."

"Shit. You could be anywhere in that old barn."

"A friend of mine gave me an idea when he said he could trace my cell phone signal to my corpse. They send one even when they're turned off. Tell that to the cops."

"What if they take it away from you?"

"The kidnappers? They probably will, but the principle still works unless they heave it across the infield."

"If they do that, I may have to go in."

"Call for backup first."

He picked up the check then. "It looks like you're working for free. What's your end?"

"The job started out straightforward, then took a mean slice. Technically, I'm still working it, so this is found money to do what I've been doing right along. Considering I've got a better than even chance of getting killed, it looks like a sound investment."

"What about this friend you mentioned?"

"He's got twice as many guts as I have, but only half the legs."

"This woman they took; she a friend?"

"Just a casual acquaintance who doesn't approve of me very much. I get a lot of that. Right now she's the only connection I've got to the end of the job I started. It would be nice if I got her out alive, but it's not my main concern."

"You're a liar. I think you're the kind of idiot they used to write songs about until people got wise there wasn't any such thing."

"You can write one about me if you want."

He put the check back on the towel and pushed it toward me. "It's a long time till dark. You should buy yourself a new suit and a four-course meal."

"You're turning me down?"

"No way. If we both come out of this, I expect you to be a character witness at my trial."

I got to Mary Ann Thaler's office in the MacNamara Federal Building just as she was locking up. "Late lunch?"

"They don't feed us at this level. I've got a meeting with the FBI special agent in charge." She wore slacks and a loose linen jacket with a shoulder bag half the size of the one she'd used to lug around heroin. "Got something to report?"

"I just wanted to ask when you go home."

"Planning on asking me out?"

"I don't date women who can outshoot me. I wanted to know if you'd be available tonight after dark."

"It still sounds like a date."

"There may be entertainment involved, but I'm not too crazy about the cover charge. I'd owe you a favor if you hung around town a couple of hours past quitting and kept your cell charged up."

"What's the ruckus?"

"That's classified for now."

"What favor can I expect in return?"

"Second prize is I won't ask you any more favors."

"What's the first prize?"

"Appointment to full marshal, if the cards fall just right."

"When do they ever? Would this have anything to do with some misplaced dope?"

"I'm not sure it's misplaced. But yeah."

She glanced at a watch with a large face and boldface numerals. Tiny elegant ladies' watches had no place in law enforcement. "I'd run the riddle out, but I'm late. Sun sets around six. I'll give you till seven-thirty for your call."

"I probably won't be the one making it. If a strange number comes up, don't leave it for voice mail."

"It isn't like you to partner up."

"I don't usually go to the government for help, either. It's the season for breaking precedent."

"This exclusive to the U.S. Marshals? No locals?"

"What happened to the joint operation?"

"Too many meetings. Like the one I'm late for."

"If that's how you want it."

"That's how it is." She left, heels snapping on the linoleum. I let her take the elevator down alone. I didn't want to take the chance of spilling my guts in a tiny enclosed space.

John Alderdyce wasn't at his desk. A civilian clerk said the inspector was out on a call. I asked when he was expected back.

"Ten minutes. Tomorrow, maybe. He's not delivering pizza."

The clerk was slight, in his twenties, half an inch short of the department minimum for police training. His face had set in an expression of sour resignation. I gave him the weary smile. "Okay, Sunshine. I'll hang around. Go back and sit by the scanner."

I sneaked part of a cigarette sitting in a chair outside the office until a woman in a sergeant's uniform got downwind of it and stuck a glass ashtray under my nose. I put it out and made do with the asbestos in the ceiling.

Alderdyce came along twenty minutes later, whistling. He stopped when I stood up. "I knew this mood was too good to last."

"Plans tonight?" I asked.

"My wife's been after me to check out the new MGM Grand. Last time we went gambling, we had to go to Windsor. That's how long it's been since we went out."

"The Grand'll still be there tomorrow night."

He spread his feet and rolled his big shoulders under his silk suit coat, assuming a slugger's stance.

"You may get a call tonight," I said, "after dark."

"About?"

"The freak snowstorm we've been having."

"You don't quit, do you? You're like an eight-day clock."

"Chances are the call will come from someone you don't know. It'll be quick, to cut down on your response time."

"Have you ever asked yourself why there's no pension plan for staked goats?"

"I can't afford to retire anyway. We on?"

"If it's a police case. I never thought I'd say it, but I'm sick of looking at Mary Ann Thaler."

"Agreed. Not the part about looking at Thaler," I added. "You married guys are too complacent."

"I may not be married after tonight. This better not be a bad tip. Who's calling?"

"Someone who's in even worse trouble than I am."

"Poor bastard. Just how far am I going after we hang up?"

"Not far, and you shouldn't run into traffic. Nobody goes there anymore."

He thought about asking more questions, shook his head a quarter inch, and unlocked the door to his office. "I got those prints back from Johnny Toledo's whiz-bang camera. Care to check out the competition?"

"Does he have vertical lines shaved in his eyebrows?"

His fist tightened on the doorknob. "You met him?"

"No. Someone did his homework."

"Stackpole. You run your own irregular police force, don't you?"

"He says it's a gang thing in China. He's here on kind of a work visa."

"Times have changed. They used to come to Detroit for professional help." He flipped on the overhead light, thumbed his way down from the top of a stack on his work table, and slid out a folder that looked like all the rest, with nothing written on the tab for guidance; his system appeared to be largely psychic in nature. From it he skinned an eight-by-ten sheet of grainy photo paper and handed it to me. "Keep it. I'm just back from faxing copies to every police agency in the state and the FBI in Washington."

I took it, wondering if that was the reason for Thaler's meeting with the local special agent in charge.

It was the same balletic pose, but the details were easier to make out in the larger format. The Asian's face was age-less, probably young, but had a plastic sheen, as if he'd had extensive work done. The razor tracks in his eyebrows were thin, invisible in the original tiny image, and ruler straight:

five in the right, four in the left. Barry was always right about the things I wanted him to be wrong about. He wore his hair collar length.

"See anything significant, Sherlock?" asked Alderdyce.

"Red stain on his heel. I'm guessing he didn't step in nail polish."

"Might as well have, unless we find the shoe. What else?"

"You mean the face work?"

"We're canvassing plastic surgeons by way of the AMA, but I don't expect anything. It looks like the slipshod work they do in China. I mean he isn't wearing a watch, or jewelry of any kind. No bulge to go with keys or change in his pockets. No *pockets*, so far as I can tell. Nothing to catch the light or snag on his clothes or jingle or slow him down."

"SOP in combat situations." I stroked a corner with a thumb. "No keys means a wheel man to take him to and from."

"Unless he keeps a hide-a-key stuck to the car."

"Not in Johnny's neighborhood. The locals can frisk a car from roof to wheel covers in three minutes. Thanks, John. I think I'll know him." I rolled up the picture and stuck it inside my sport coat.

"Hang on." He conjured up a flimsy sheet of pinkish paper from another stack. "Sign this."

It was a receipt for personal property. While I was reading it he circled behind the table, plucked a Ziploc bag from a shallow drawer, and dropped it on top of the mountain of paper and cardboard. I signed the sheet, gave it back, and transferred my .38 Chief's Special from the bag to my belt. I thanked him again.

"Just reload it before you go wherever it is you're going. We recycle the ammo."

I went to the Hockeytown Cafe for a late lunch, not for the food but for the noise and company. I didn't taste what I ate and when I left I didn't remember what I'd ordered. In the office I cleaned the fat cop thumbprints off the revolver, applied oil, wiped off the excess, and loaded all the chambers from the box I kept in the safe. The process brightened my outlook a little; the Luger was reliable, but it handled like borrowed property and I didn't like the action.

I put it aside and went through the mail. I opened a letter from a party I'd known pretty well for a while, but it read like something written by someone I'd bumped up against on a cruise years ago. I dumped it with the rest. I burned to-bacco, tilted back in my chair with my ankles crossed on a drawleaf, and studied the photo of the man who'd killed Johnny Toledo and probably Reuben Crossgrain. It had been difficult to concentrate with a police inspector looking over my shoulder.

He was Chinese. I wondered why the plastic job. I picked up the phone to ask Barry if it was a Paper Dog thing, some kind of shape-changing ritual to isolate raw recruits from their past before training, or if it was repair work in keeping with the rough-and-tumble nature of the occupation; but I thought Barry would just pester me about letting him ride along that night. I cradled the receiver.

I was glad now I'd decided to keep the office dry. There are plenty of excuses to drink. Boredom is one of the most com-mon. The odds against me hardly needed help. I smoked, napped, typed up some surveillance reports I'd had hanging, filed the carbons, and stacked the originals for mailing. I still felt drowsy, from a combination of irregular hours and adrenaline highs and lows. I smashed water into my face in the little water closet and let it trickle down inside my collar while I stood at the window to watch the traffic beginning to clot two stories down for the four-hour rush hour. It gave me glimpses of crepey orange-and-black party deocrations piled in back seats and the occasional tiny passenger dressed up like Harry Potter. We were all waiting for the sun to go down.

Gale Kreski drove a commercial panel truck with no windows in the back, probably to discourage thieves from spotting the musical equipment he would carry often; a magnetic rubber sign on the side of the cab read LI'L TREASURES DAY CARE for camouflage. He honked in front of my building and I went downstairs, chewing pills. The .38 rode low on my back under the tail of my sport coat.

Outside, the street lamps had just come on: Mosquitoes, gnats, and the odd little brown bat circled the globes. I rode with him a block and a half down to the lot where I parked the Cutlass and went over the instructions on the way. We checked to make sure our cell batteries were working, the modern equivalent of synchronizing watches. No need for that with all of them feeding off the same atomic clock. His ponytail spilled out over the adjustable band of a dark figureless cap and he'd tugged on a dull blue sweatshirt over his tattoos.

Parking in Corktown wasn't a problem at that hour. The family places did most of their business toward the end of the week and the Irish saloons where mayors and governors were elected in a time of more innocent corruption were boarded up. Roving bands of pirates hawking nonsanctioned pennants and key chains had migrated downtown when the

Tigers deserted their century-old home for Comerica Park. Kreski slid into the curb two spaces behind me, shut down his motor, and sat in darkness. I left my car unlocked for reasons of expedience and walked two blocks down to the Corner.

Michigan and Trumbull, and on it the dog bowl–shaped pile of brick and cement where Cobb and Greenburg and Kaline and Horton, Tramell, Whitaker, and all the other immortals had thrown and slugged and run bases from the first major league game in baseball history until free agency and skyrocketing payrolls gave the game to the corporations. Their statues in Comerica Park were made of stuff less permanent than their phantoms'. With the floodlights shut down and looted of their copper and silver, the building seemed darker than night.

The first gate I came to was chained and padlocked. It would be the same at all the others. I scaled the chain link and let myself down on the other side. I felt like a kid sneaking in to catch the last couple of innings. The passage beyond was flanked by block walls with leprous patches of bare concrete gnawing through the dark paint. A waist-high iron railing installed to funnel the crowds toward ticket-takers was scabbed with rust, icy to the touch; the skeleton of the old park was asserting itself through the rotting flesh. Something glistening slithered into a patch of greasy moonlight before a low breeze. I recoiled, but it was nothing more sinister than a fresh condom wrapper. The old barn hadn't been abandoned entirely.

I strained my nostrils for the reassuring smells of mustard and sauerkraut and old cooking oil, but even their ghosts had decamped, leaving behind a sour assurance of mildew.

The place felt and smelled like an unused basement. It reminded me unpleasantly of the scene of Reuben Crossgrain's massacre.

The recesses behind the concession counters were empty and black: no more five-dollar hot dogs, no bobble-head dolls to tear apart at an eight-year-old's inquisitive hand. I found my way to the base of the steps leading to the seats, rested a hand on the .38, and climbed, up to the top where by day and by floodlight the green of the infield had glowed like Kryptonite, with men in white livery playing a boys' game of catch; now it lay shaggy and dark in a sharp angle of illumination, and beyond that dead black. All the seats that had ringed the field of play, even the bleachers, had been scavenged by vandals or sold by the management to souvenir hunters. The empty tiers had acquired a kind of ruined elegance through their absence, alone among the park's features; they might have belonged to the Colosseum in Rome.

I felt more alone than I ever had. I was an astronaut marooned on a dead planet, billions of light years from home. I didn't know if I was early or too late.

"Hello?"

No response, not even an echo. The two syllables had fallen dead on the top step.

I cupped my hands around my mouth and shouted at the top of my lungs. "Hello!"

This time it rang, wobbling around the perimeter like the first line of "The Star Spangled Banner" and a thousand names forgotten and sent back to the minors. It had the tinny quality of stage thunder.

"There's no need to tax your vocal cords, Mr. Walker. The

acoustics here are quite marvelous. Impressive, actually, for so young a civilization."

The voice was a smooth contralto, planed all around until no trace remained of a regional accent, not even generic American. Mocking, for all that. I knew it as well as my own, and it carried nothing but chill dread.

I waited years, feeling the weight of them in the pause. At length a shadow separated itself from the black at the opposite end of the stadium, stretching from the visitors' dugout nearly to the pitcher's mound, what was left of it; towing a tiny figure that as it advanced in my direction seemed to fill the vast empty space until I felt like backing away to give it room: a small, feminine shape despite the mannish tailoring of its dress, and one that in the paranoia of the waking night I'd hoped never to see again.

PART FOUR

THE GARDENS OF MADAM SING

TWENTY-FIVE

The last time I'd seen Charlotte Sing, we'd been several miles over Buffalo, New York, and closing the distance fast. It had been in a cargo plane with a refrigerated hold containing several hundred million dollars' worth of human organs bound for the European and Asian black market and one dead body scheduled for disposal in the North Atlantic; me, too, I'd suspected, but the plane had crashed before that could be established, and Madam Sing vanished.

She was the product of an American serviceman and an illiterate South Korean girl during the U.S. Police Action, but cosmetic surgery and rigorous diet and exercise took twenty years off her appearance. From what I could see from my position halfway up to the nosebleed section, two years as a fugitive from international justice hadn't added so much as a wrinkle. Small-boned and straight, in a dark suit cut to play down the swell of her breasts and her girlish waist, she placed one modest heel in front of the other, crossing the ragged turf of the diamond as if it were a polished floor.

She stopped short of home plate with her hands folded

demurely in front of her: a tiny thing, five feet and less than a hundred pounds, but a heavyweight on the Most Wanted list. She'd come to the United States a slave, toiling as an unpaid prostitute in massage parlors, and parlayed what she'd learned into an executive position in the flesh-peddling market worldwide, billions in undeclared income, section upon section of real estate leased on the up-and-up to brothels and gambling hells—her legitimate front—and a crackpot plan to flood the Free World with illegal aliens. She had brains to spare, but they'd gone rotten on a steady diet of hate.

"MacArthur Industries." I spoke in a level tone now. She was right about the sound quality in the stadium; you could hear a peanut vendor's cry above the cheers from a grand slam. "The name kept needling me, just not enough to make the connection. You once said you used it to check into hotels because General MacArthur was the first American to leave Korea."

"It was a beautiful country before he came, he and his gum-chewing G.I. hordes; steeped in ancient tradition and unpolluted by Western decadence. He left it a shabby little border town filled with pidgin English and cheap trinkets manufactured by our enemies in Japan. 'Police Action.'" Her tone smirked. "Just who appointed the Pentagon to direct traffic everywhere in the world?"

"Yeah. There was that business of North Korea burning down whole villages in South Korea and conscripting the surviving boys to serve in the Communist army, but what the hell."

"Worse was happening in Argentina and Jerusalem, and in your own South. I don't question your government's tendency to butt in anywhere it chooses so much as the arbitrary nature of its choices."

"It's your government, too. Last I heard you were still a citizen, subject to our laws."

"For the moment. Revocation and deportation are under discussion, and may have already taken place in absentia. If I were returned to Korea under my own name, I would be executed in a week. Certain of my activities in Asia are in violation of the laws in North and South. Obviously, I am not here legally. I stand before you a woman without a country."

"You're exaggerating. I'm pretty sure you're not wanted in Antarctica."

" 'Wanted.' The only one-word oxymoron in the limited English language. The people who apply it to me would be contented if I would simply go away."

"I'm with them, just as soon as I get what I came for."

"And yet you came empty-handed. Were my instructions not clear?"

"The boxes are in a safe place. Just when did you know you'd be dealing with me?"

"After the death of Johnny Toledo. Once you'd entered the picture, connecting you with Reuben Crossgrain was simple conjecture. I know you've been playing man-in-the-middle with the police and the federal government. You'd be surprised, or perhaps not, to learn just how much cooperation one can buy if she can afford the market rate. You Americans are so self-destructively cynical that it's difficult to bring you to shock or outrage. Rome fell under similar circumstances."

"Took it five hundred years."

"Things move so much faster now. Do you imagine it's revenge I'm after?"

"It occurred to me. I cost you some change a couple of years back."

"Money is a disposable commodity, and an unlimitedly renewable resource, like people. You learn these things in the sex trade. Your sorry life is the best revenge I could expect, if I cared about such things. We're both here to complete a simple transaction."

"Alone?"

"I am alone always. If you mean am I unaccompanied, no." She lifted her voice an octave, in a language I will never understand.

Suddenly I knew I wasn't alone either. The shadows to my left gathered into a solid mass, dressed all in dark fabrics so that the pallid face seemed to float, a disembodied head. It was an old spiritualists' trick, but in those surroundings and in the presence of that diminutive ogre in the infield it made me jump just the same.

"Shau Win Chang." That eerily aethnic contralto isolated the three syllables in such a way that I recognized it as a formal introduction. I insist on nothing less when it comes to people who murder people with their limbs alone.

TWENTY-SIX

Disarm him. Inspect him for wires."

He stood silent following the quiet command, his arms down at his sides, watching me with eyes shaped like inverted commas. The cuts in his eyebrows looked like marks on a tally sheet—or notches on an old-time gunfighter's six-gun. Chang's calm seemed ancient, but then all I had to compare it with was the rictus he'd worn in his photograph, snapped in a moment of violent action. In his dark, close-fitting clothes he was built straight up and down, like a pipe cleaner. I wondered again about the stiff artificial sheen of his features, like new skin showing where a severe sunburn had peeled away.

As I reached for the revolver behind my back, he shifted his weight onto one foot. I'd seen the other foot raised and what it had done to Johnny Toledo. I held the gun out by the barrel. "Your picture doesn't do you justice."

He hesitated, a crease disturbing the balloonlike smoothness of his forehead. It flattened out as from an effort. Something glittered in one eye. He knew what I'd been talking about. He took the .38 and groped inside my coat with his free hand, all the way down to my groin.

"Now his wireless."

I thought about saying I didn't have one, but I knew nothing about her sources. I had a hunch Chang was short-tempered for all his training. He took the cell from my hand.

"Destroy it."

He bent to place it on the step he was standing on and raised his heel. I kicked at his head.

I'd made better decisions. He ducked my foot almost in slow motion, a sharp contrast to the blow that struck me full in the chest. I didn't see it coming, and it came so fast I wasn't sure if it came from a fist or a foot. I have the impression my heart stopped. I spun, vaguely aware that if I didn't I would fall head first and backward down the steps onto the concrete floor at the base. I barked my ribs on the iron railing, closed my hand around it, and waited an agonizing moment for my lungs to reinflate. They filled with a long hoarse draft and a thin splinter of pure pain that felt as if my breastbone had torn loose of the shallow layer of flesh that covered it.

"That was imbecilic, even for you," Charlotte Sing said.

"I regretted it right away." I doubt she heard me. It came out in a hollow whisper. I'd already taken a steering column in the same spot.

Chang's long hair had spilled over one eye. He swept it back with a flirt of his head, lifted his foot again, and brought it down hard on my cell. It flew into four pieces. He swung open the cylinder of my revolver, tipped the cartridges out onto his palm, and tossed them over his shoulder. They rattled down the risers toward the backstop. He flipped the cylinder back into place and stuck the weapon out at me. I took it and returned it to its clip. He watched me with an expression of contempt.

I found my voice then. "Does he speak? I'm pretty sure he doesn't roll over and play dead."

"His English is spotty. He hasn't been here long, and he prefers not to appear foolish; a vanity you don't share. I take it you know something of the Society of the Paper Dog."

"Everything but the face job."

"A precaution, in his particular division. Every step is taken to prevent the authorities from tracing them back to their families in the event of capture. Shau Win Chang is not his birth name, of course."

"I didn't think it suited him."

"The surgery is conducted without anesthesia, which is the final test before each man is allowed out into the world. Some don't survive."

Chang's posture straightened a half inch; it hadn't been anything like a stoop to begin with. He'd followed that part of the conversation.

"Now that we're caught up," I said.

She said something in Chinese. Chang backed down a step toward the infield and to the side. I started down that way. The hairs lifted on the back of my neck as he followed.

At the bottom, he touched my arm, steering me to the right. We circled a third of the way around the playing surface and entered a tunnel leading to the home team locker room. The floor sloped down into ocean-floor blackness. Here the mildew stench that stalked the building acquired a texture of its own: Athlete's-foot spores mingled with shower mold and the residue in toilets and urinals left unscrubbed after the final game, years now in the past. The acrid sweat of a million trips around the bases was sunk deep in the block walls. I put a palm against one for guidance and the rough damp surface chilled me to the base of my spine. Chang followed, directed by some GPS all his own.

The darkness was complete, but as I continued, groping my way with my feet and holding a hand out in front of me to keep from colliding with any of the variety of hard elements that went into the stadium's construction, I grew aware of a source of light ahead. It spared me from banging a shin against a long bench bolted to the floor, an oblong impression in the dim glow. The steel lockers that had stood on either side were gone, pried loose by thieves or sold legitimately at auction to sports buffs. The garage sale was winding down; there was little left to do but knock over the rest, and that, too, would be peddled off piece by piece, inert chunks of masonry holding down stacks of paper in someone's office.

The light grew less dim. I followed it through a rectangular arch into a small square room, concrete on two sides, with a partition separating it from the locker room with large square openings in it where there had been glass panes. The door had been taken down. I hoped it had brought a fair market price. Managers from George Stallings to Sparky Anderson had closed it to inform five generations of players that they'd been cut from the lineup.

There was a strong smell of kerosene, and the hissing and popping of a badly trimmed wick inside the smudged glass chimney of a lantern burning on the floor. The office had been gutted of fixtures and furniture. A white resin patio chair had been brought in, presumably to tie its occupant to and prevent her escape.

"Please."

Her voice was hoarse, and I wondered if she'd gotten the same treatment from Chang that I had. Ouida wore a light printed blouse soaked through at the armpits and a gray tailored skirt that looked as if it belonged to a suit. She was in stocking feet with runners. Plastic zip ties, the kind electricians use to corral bundles of wire, fastened her ankles to the legs of her chair and her arms were drawn behind the back and probably bound the same way. Her mascara had bled down her cheeks and her bright red hair looked more unnatural than it did in Eugenia Pappas' house. In that bleak place, any dash of color might have come from outer space.

"She's been fed and watered. Toilet facilities have been arranged, and exercise to aid circulation. The setting is ideal. There was no need to gag her after she was brought here. Who is to hear her cries for help?"

Charlotte Sing stood with her back to a solid wall, arms crossed. In the unsteady light she looked even younger than usual; her small stature and fine features might have belonged to a teenage gymnast.

" 'Fed and watered,' " I said. "She's a human being, not a geranium. Who's been looking after her?"

"Chang and myself. I've learned from experience to pare my staff down to small departments, each assigned to one responsibility."

"He wasn't trained as a babysitter. How's he feel about it?"

"I don't poll my subordinates on the subject of their opinions. Where are my boxes?" She lifted her gaze from the captive. Her eyes were as nearly black as any I'd seen. Nocturnal animals in photographs were as close as it got; but their eyes were almost all pupil. I couldn't tell where her irises left off and the pupils began. It was like staring down two deep shafts you knew weren't empty at the bottom.

I looked away and smiled at Ouida, as much to cover my retreat as to reassure her. "Eugenia's worried. She gave me a fat bonus to bring you back in good health."

"Did she say why?" The rawness of her voice was painful. I decided she'd broken it shouting for help. There were no marks visible and she didn't seem to be in shock.

"She wants to use you as a bargaining chip with God."

After a long moment she nodded, with ironic twists at the corners of her lips. "Thank you for being honest. She's told me her grand plan for salvation."

I returned my attention to Madam Sing. "They're in my car. You can have them. They're too rich for my blood."

"I'll take that as a compliment. I knew you'd open them and look inside. The poppies that produced the alkaloid to make the original opium are mutations, genetically enhanced. The standard plant requires at least twelve hours of sunlight per day to produce blossoms; the altered variety needs only six. This means it can be grown in temperate climates, not just the tropics."

"My mother used to grow them in Michigan in the summer," I said. "To look at, not to stick in her veins."

"Had she access to these plants, she could have seen them bloom from May to November. In addition to a protracted season, the plants themselves are half again as fertile. My enforced retirement has made me quite the gardener." Satirical humor sounded mechanical in those lathed tones. "The heroin that's caused the local authorities so much work is not even the pure form. Without adulteration, a grain would produce euphoria; two would result in death. A single kilogram in its original form would slay every addict in North America."

"When did you start working for the DEA?"

"Obviously, the quality of the shipment that reached Detroit was reduced. It would be counterproductive to destroy the market in one fell swoop."

"So it's a fund-raiser. I heard your assets were seized or frozen." I shook my head. "I have to say I'm disappointed. The Charlotte Sing I knew wasn't in it for the money."

"Obtaining wealth is a talent. If you work at it, you can turn it into a skill. I can raise a quarter billion dollars' credit in twenty-four hours on my reputation alone; not in the legitimate commodities market, of course, but the dollar goes just as far. Farther, some places. What's become of America's image in the world community is a scandal."

"Our dollar's not doing so well, either. I thought you might have given up on destroying our culture with undocumented immigrants. We slurp them up like Pepsi, even built a statue to advertise it."

"I disagree, but I never till the same field twice. Insanity is defined as the expectation of achieving a different result from a tactic that failed the first time."

"This one failed big. You or one of your people let the heroin out of the bag in a part of America that destroyed itself without your help a long time ago."

She showed something then; smugness, or surprise—disappointment? Had I stumbled too easily into a hole she'd dug? She liked me a little despite herself or I wouldn't have survived our last meeting. Maybe she expected better of me. Oh, she was insane. But then I decided I'd tried to get too much out of a change of expression in bad light.

"I don't reward mistakes," she said, "but my policy is to let everyone have at least one. Failure is education." She slid a slender hand into a side pocket in her coat and drew out a clasp knife with a red lacquer handle. "Will you do the honors? Taking her with you will spare you an extra trip after you lead Chang to those boxes."

I hesitated, then took the knife from her cool palm, pried loose the blade, and went behind Ouida's chair to saw through the ties on her wrists. I couldn't believe it was as easy as all that. One of these days I'm going to have to learn to trust my instincts.

When I freed her ankles, Chang snatched the knife from my hand, nicking my palm, and gave it to his boss, who folded and returned it to her pocket. I rose and helped Ouida to her feet. She swayed; I caught and held her while the circulation returned to her hands and feet. She was warm and soft, but steel-reinforced at the center. She'd survive—depending on what else was in store. Her breath caught in tearless sobs.

"I have something else to show you before you go."

I looked at Sing. "I didn't come for the tour."

"No extra charge." Her speech was a crazy mix of Oxford English and carnival barker. She spoke rapidly to Chang, who bent and lifted the hissing lantern from the floor. That shift from warrior to redcap must have been a severe test of his discipline. I wondered if I could profit from that.

We followed him through the door and deeper into the building, Ouida leaning on me, Sing behind us. I squeezed her hand. It was cold, but no limp fish. At that point I was grasping at anything.

Greasy orange light slung shadows into shapes that crawled

along walls of block and poured concrete. The air was clammy cold, with the stale smell of an unventilated bunker.

In the curve of the wall someone, a player or other club employee, had sprayed an exuberant "1968" in numerals three feet high, faded now like its spirit. That was the year after the great riot, the Tigers' first championship in twenty-three years. The victory had been interpreted as a sign of hope in a season of despair; in those days, any bright omen at all was solid currency. No one could have predicted that forty years later the despair would still be in place. It wasn't the building's fault. They're only as good as the people who stream through them.

Another doorless opening led into the equipment room, where Chang waited with the lantern hanging down at his side. It meant nothing to him, that room of golden fleeces and enchanted swords. He'd known places more ancient and far more fabled and been conditioned to disregard them as dead fossils. To him the ceramic army was so much superstition to be pulverized for standing room for those of flesh and blood. I hated him then nonobjectively, like a stubborn nail that wouldn't drive. There may have been a normal upbringing there, on the other side of the face job and desensitizing, but to me he was just an arrangement of pulleys and gears that made my hands thirsty for a monkey wrench to throw into the middle of it. A gasp from Ouida told me I'd gripped her arm to the point of bruising. I relaxed my grip.

The space we were in was three times the size of the manager's office. Although the bats and gloves and helmets and shinguards and catchers' gear were gone, the racks and steel utility shelves remained, the shelves standing in parallel rows like library stacks. They were nothing without the postgame chatter, the sports clichés and split infinitives and smell of ferment from spilled champagne when a pennant went down. A building is just mortar and reinforcing rods without human input. It was long past time to put it out of its pain. I'd push the plunger myself if they'd let me.

Charlotte Sing said something to Chang, who led the way along the ends of the stacks. Coming to the last one he stopped and stepped aside, still holding the lantern low so that only a circle of floor was visible in its light. A puddle of seepage lay there, incubating mosquito larvae. At the opposite end of the stack, shadows formed a heap in the alcove formed by the wall and the steel structure. It might have been a pile of equipment that had been left behind.

"I'm understaffed," Charlotte Sing said. "Security at the borders has limited me to Chang and a few dozen day laborers recruited locally, with as little explanation as possible about the reason for their employment. In the absence of physical force I considered it necessary to take other steps to secure your cooperation."

She spoke again in Chinese. Chang raised the lantern to shoulder height. The light penetrated the blackness.

A folding cot had been erected in the narrow space at the end. I left Ouida to support herself against the wall while I went in to identify the small figure stretched out on the cot.

It was Luis Quincy Adams, Johnny Toledo's errand boy, eyes closed, face sheathed in cold sweat. Something crunched underfoot when I moved in to see if he was breathing. I withdrew my foot and looked down at the broken pieces of a disposable syringe.

TWENTY-SEVEN

I couldn't tell if he was breathing. When I placed the back of my hand near his lips, nothing stirred the hairs. I lifted his bare arm from atop the thin wool blanket that covered him and pressed my thumb to the artery on the underside of his wrist. I felt nothing at first, then a shallow throb. I lowered the arm.

"The mildest of injections," Charlotte Sing said. "Just enough to keep him unconscious. I shouldn't need to add that the solution will be increased substantially if despite Chang's supervision you fail to return with the converter boxes, but certain things are safer not left unsaid."

I asked how long he'd been there.

"Chang found him at the bus station yesterday, on his own initiative. He couldn't fly without photo ID, and you can no longer board a train without passing through security. It was possible the authorities had been notified, with his description. He had a ticket to El Paso."

"He was on his way to Mexico."

"Your advice. No, we didn't torture him. He told us about

you and the camera phone he gave you, but that was under the influence of the drug. I assume by now you've turned the phone over to the police."

"He's just a kid."

"At his age I'd been a slave for two years. Children sometimes endure under circumstances that would destroy their elders."

Ouida made a noise. I'd almost forgotten about her. "You don't need the boy," I said. "He doesn't know anything the cops don't."

"He can give evidence in support of it; but I'm not interested in holding him. When I have those boxes, Chang and I will leave. By the time you bring back help, we'll be out of U.S. jurisdiction."

That meant Canada; and I knew then Detroit had been no accident. It was only three minutes across the border by bridge and tunnel, only they wouldn't be using either. The guards on either side couldn't be expected to catch every small watercraft, every private plane or helicopter. She could slip out as easily as she'd slipped in.

I stood facing her in the crawling light. "Neat but sloppy. Those temps you hired spilled a lot of powder on the street."

"Oh, we always meant to measure the impact in a real-world situation. The boxes containing the heroin were intended to stray into the hands of local dealers. I overestimated their ability to recognize its purity and adulterate it properly; I've been away, and I'm still a novice in this area of commerce. Product development claimed most of my attention. The inferior quality of the Mexican import came as a shock.

"When the deaths began to attract the attention of the media, I issued instructions to reclaim as much of the shipment as possible. Your Mr. Crossgrain was a clerical mistake, made by an employee in a computer boiler room. He provided a tax identification number with his order that was similar to one on our list of customers in the related field of smuggled electronics. I came here to correct that error and make sure that no others took place."

"With Chang."

"We traveled separately; but yes. The local pool of qualified professionals is polluted with undercover officers."

"Was Johnny Toledo on your customer list?"

"He was a parasite. I'm sure it wasn't your intention, when you made contact with him, to set him off after those boxes, but that was the result. By the time my people learned they'd been recalled, they were already on the street."

I'd guessed part of that. The rest was news. "So it wasn't your people who burgled Crossgrain's place the first time?"

She laughed unexpectedly, a tinkle of bells that walked up my spine like a centipede. "I'm not the only criminal in town. The fools who stole that shipment never looked inside. They marketed them at the going rate for hot merchandise." Her face smoothed. "We've managed to recover only fourteen boxes. The ten we tracked to Eugenia Pappas' warehouse leave one unaccounted for. I assume that found its way into official hands or you wouldn't have known heroin was involved."

I didn't see any reason to tell her how Rudy the street person had swiped one from Johnny. "I'm back to what's in it for you, if not the cash."

"That isn't part of our transaction. The boxes, please." When I glanced at Luis she said, "He'll be here when you return."

I looked at Chang waiting, standing as motionless as the

fixtures with the lantern raised, the light reflecting off the skin grafts on his face and the dark glossy marbles of his eyes.

Just then the boy on the cot made a low whimpering noise and stirred. Charlotte Sing came forward, drawing a slim leather case from the pocket opposite the one where she kept the knife.

"Don't be alarmed," she said, spreading it open on the boy's chest. "This is methadone. Too sudden an awakening from the other can trigger cardiac arrest." She filled one of a row of disposable syringes from one of a pair of small prescription bottles with different colored labels and squirted a short arc of liquid to clear the barrel of air. "The second bottle contains morphine, distilled from the opium from my gardens. You know the sound quality in this building. Any disturbance you've planned will lead to tragedy."

She lifted his arm from the blanket. Ouida turned her face to the wall.

Chang accepted a loose key from his mistress and directed me with grunts and gestures to a different gate from the one I'd climbed before. I stood supporting Ouida while he bent over the padlock and undid the chain. We preceded him through the opening.

It was a hike from there to the Cutlass, supporting most of the young woman's weight on my shoulders, but as we came under the street lamp nearest the car I managed to turn her between us and made a cutting gesture on the offside with my hand at waist level. Gale Kreski's panel truck was dark, parked in the gloom between lamps; I hoped he was paying attention. If he called Alderdyce and Thaler as we'd discussed, the Chinese would react at the first sound of a rapidly approaching vehicle. I'd experienced him in action, and there had been Madam Sing's warning about what would happen to Luis.

I fumbled open the door on the passenger's side of the Cutlass and lowered Ouida onto the seat. I had to pry my arm free of her fingers. She was shaking violently with post-trauma, her teeth rattling. I guided her legs in their ruined stockings into the car, patted her thigh, and closed the door on her.

Chang stood within lunging room as I unlocked and swung open the trunk. When I bent to lift a stack of boxes, he grunted and waved toward the street. He must have had instructions. I backed into the traffic lane, arms spread, while he scooped up a box in both hands.

I had an instant before he realized it was too light to contain a kilo of heroin. He was making a noise of surprise when I slammed the trunk down on his head.

That was the plan; but he had the reflexes of a scalded cat. He blocked the lid with his arm and it bounced back up off his biceps. At the same time he braced himself on the bumper with his other hand and his leg swung around on ball bearings, catching me on the bone at the side of my knee with the edge of his foot. Shards of blue-white pain shot out in all directions. The street slammed into me before I knew I was folding.

All this happened fast. What happened next was faster. I'd landed hard on my shoulder. I rolled over onto my back to defend myself from the next attack. The empty revolver dug into my tailbone. I needed cartridges. I needed thunderbolts from heaven. Chang bent his knees to leap.

An engine roared. Rubber shrieked. Something as big as a building hurtled along the curb. I rolled again to clear myself from its path. I came to rest on my face just as something struck something else with the thud of a baseball bat colliding with a side of beef. A high thin scream pierced the echo of torn tires.

I got a palm on the pavement and pushed myself up onto my good leg. Everything is relative; it had been my bad leg until a moment ago. Chang's face was a mask of agony, and then it was gone. He slumped forward over the boxes in the trunk. He could fall no farther. His legs were pinned between the Cutlass' rear bumper and the front bumper of Kreski's truck.

"Ogodogodogodogodogodogodogodogodogodogod."

This went on as I hobbled around to curbside and snatched open the passenger's door. It cut off on the instant. I took Ouida's chin and turned her face toward me. Her eyes were white around the irises and a shadow was spreading under the skin of her forehead where it had struck the padded dash, but that seemed to be the extent of the damage.

Well, I'd have cried too. I smiled at her, watching the hysteria fade. She rested her cheek on the back of my hand. After a moment she nodded and I shut her back in.

Kreski was standing outside his cab. His cell phone screen glowed in one hand. His thumb twitched toward a button.

"Hang on," I said.

He lifted the thumb. "New plan?"

"I never really cared for the first one." I frowned. "I brought you in for hand-to-hand combat. I didn't say anything about a lead foot."

He grinned, an event as rare as solar eclipse. "Yeah, well, what're you gonna do? It's Detroit."

TWENTY-EIGHT

When Kreski backed up his truck, Chang slid into a pile on the street. I approached him carefully, but his whirling-dervish days were over; he'd need braces in the exercise yard. The bump had shattered both legs as thoroughly as he had any of his victims'. He was breathing shallowly, whistling in his throat when he exhaled. Barely conscious.

Kreski stood over us. "We can't leave him like this."

"You're right. Get something to tie him up."

"I meant a hospital."

"A boy inside needs it more. This one can still crawl. You want to wonder where he is a year from now when the bones knit?"

He trotted over to his truck and cane back with a coil of piano wire. Disregarding Chang's gasps I dragged him over to the street lamp, heaved him into a sitting position with his back against the base—he screamed—and wired his wrists together on the other side.

Kreski watched me tie off the wire. I made it bite. "He'll slash himself to the bone if he tries to get loose."

"That's the idea." I snatched the cutters from Kreski's hand and snipped the coil free. My hands shook. I was going through some post-trauma of my own.

"You okay?"

"I'm a little worked up." I staggered to my feet and gave him back the wires and cutters. "I need you to take Ouida home."

"What about you?"

"I've got to get the boy."

"Who's in there with him?"

"Just one person. A woman."

"A *woman's* behind all this?"

"If you knew this woman you wouldn't be surprised."

He helped me take Ouida from the car and went ahead to wait by the truck. She seemed steadier now, taking some weight off me. "I—I have the impression I was unkind to you." I had to strain to hear her.

"I bring that out in people."

"That horrible woman. Is she—?"

"The Queen of Cuckoo? She belongs in a Saturday morning cartoon. That's where we keep the really dangerous ones."

"Do you think she knows something went wrong?"

"I don't know. If sound travels through the walls the way it does inside, yeah."

"What will you do?"

"Wait for the cops," Kreski said. He took Ouida's arm gently. The other slid through my hand, paused when our palms touched. I squeezed hers quickly and let go. He helped her up onto the seat beside the driver's.

"Can't," I said. "Give it fifteen minutes, then call both numbers I gave you. Tell them to come to the equipment room. Someone must have a plan of the building. Fifteen," I repeated. "I want her in reach before she hears so much as a hinge squeak." I showed him the revolver.

"Shouldn't you reload?"

"I didn't bring extra shells."

"What are you going to do, throw it at her?"

"That's what they do in movies."

"You just make this up as you go along?"

"It makes itself up. I just follow."

I watched the panel truck pull out, then fished out the last of the pills Barry had given me and crunched them thoughtfully. Chang breathed in broken moans, the back of his head resting against the lamppost. His ruined legs were spread out in front of him like a doll's. He didn't exist for me.

I swallowed, tasting the bitter medicine in the roots of my tongue. The Cutlass' trunk stood open. I holstered the .38 and lifted out a box containing an empty TV converter.

The gate I'd come through with Chang was still unlocked. Out in the moonlight he'd abandoned the lantern, the kerosene burning low now on the ground. I shifted the box under my arm, lifted the lamp by the bail. It lit my way only a yard at a time, but the weight of it quieted the tremors in my hand. Navigating by memory and the odd familiar feature I found my way through the building's entrails. The route back inside seemed three times as long as the way out. Twice I stopped, second-guessing myself; had I taken a wrong turn? But even a place built in so lopsided a circle led eventually to the right spot.

The opening to the equipment room made a black rectangle

in the pale wall. Was she waiting there in darkness? It was inconceivable that Charlotte Sing, who'd seen the way to freedom and power from the bottom of the human compost, hadn't made provisions for so small a comfort as a source of light. Or could she see in the dark? Maybe her eyes were all pupil after all.

I stepped inside and stopped, holding the lantern high. In that primitive cave in the center of a city of just under a million people I made a swell target for something ancient and evil.

I stepped forward. Anything was better than standing still and inviting paralysis.

Luis lay as I'd left him, rolling his head now from side to side in some restless dream. I propped the lantern on an empty utility shelf high enough to shed light down on the cot and felt again for his pulse. It seemed stronger than before; then it didn't. His young system seemed to be tiring of the struggle to survive.

"Hang on, muchacho. Those bulls in Mexico don't stand a chance." I was talking in a singsong rhythm, like someone saying grace.

He whimpered, shifted a leg under the blanket. The long muscle stood out in his thigh. He was running down some adobe-lined street.

"You're short nine boxes and one man."

The low contralto, too scrupulously separated from any hint of regionality, made me shudder. It was like coming upon a snake when you were expecting something else. I willed the tension out of my shoulders and turned around, sliding the revolver out of its holster in the same movement. Charlotte Sing stood at the other end of the narrow aisle between the wall and the rack of shelves, hands folded at her waist. Her gaze slid from the .38 to my face.

"You should consider carrying a semiautomatic pistol," she said. "The light shows through the empty chambers in a revolver."

I hung on to it anyway. From my angle I couldn't tell if that was true. "You've got about five minutes before the cops come. Plenty of time to run—if you're right about the gun."

She didn't move. "This is the second time Chang has disappointed me. It was clumsy of him to allow himself to be photographed. Did you overcome him alone?"

"I had a couple of tons of help. They can pin him back together or deport him as is. What's the appeals process for Paper Dog killers in China?"

"If you came back for the boy, why did you bring any boxes at all?"

"I thought you might like to take a look inside." I let the shipping carton fall to the floor and kicked it her way. It slid to a stop at her feet.

She remained unmoving for a moment, then bent a knee to lift it. She let it drop and rose. "Did you remove the contents?"

"I'm not sure it ever had any. How much do you trust your people?"

"They know the penalty for theft and betrayal. This is the work of the Pappas woman."

"It's possible. Her caretaker never even knew the boxes were in the warehouse. Her people could have gutted them any time and resealed the cartons while he was busy messing with his plastic models, or they might have arrived empty, having been harvested somewhere along the way. You can fund a lot of charities with twenty kilos of souped-up heroin.

After that, Ouida was intended to track down the boxes in the system and report them. Maybe she was supposed to take the fall for what was missing."

"And you consider *me* wicked."

"You and Eugenia are both as screwy as a couple of dancing caterpillars. She thinks she can buy her way into Paradise, and you think you can bring the country to its knees with an army of strung-out drug addicts."

"And how do I think I can do that?"

"I tried it out on a police inspector I know, before either of us suspected you were involved. If we had, he might've spent more time on it. As long as the dope keeps circulating, the worst thing the cops have to deal with is a hike in the mortality rate among junkies. They only get desperate when it stops. The price goes up and so does the crime rate. Once they've had a taste of that supersmack and they can't get any more, every city in the country is in for a major crime wave, the president declares martial law, and the American idea is dead for at least a generation."

"So that's my plan. It seems sound."

"I'm sure you thought so when you issued that recall. You explain too much to be a first-class liar. You didn't underestimate the impact of prime cut on a place like Detroit. You shut off the tap here to see how well it worked before you went national." I shook my head. "It isn't sound. In fact, it's shaky as hell. There's always a Eugenia Pappas, a Johnny Toledo, a donkey wrangler in the desert, or someone on your own export team on the other side of the world; some greedy little leak to spoil the grand scheme. No one can interrupt the supply when there's so much money to be made by keeping it flowing. In this case, one nut canceled out the other."

"Do you imagine you can insult me by calling me insane?"

"Lady, you're a loon. Take it or don't."

Something crashed in the distance; a gate flung open or a sledge hitting a fire door. Charlotte Sing turned her head.

I cocked the .38. The noise drew her attention back to me. I told her to hold still or I'd shoot. She smiled, shook her head, and backed into darkness. Tiny feet rattled on concrete and were gone.

TWENTY-NINE

I don't see why this man has to be here. He has no clearance."
The party's name was Messarian, or something similarly Armenian in origin, and he seemed to be flaking
away before our eyes. Whenever he shook his head, a fresh
fall of dandruff drifted to the shoulders of his charcoal-gray
suit like snow in a globe. I never got his title or which Cabinet department he was with, but he gave the impression of
having something to do with Homeland Security and Immi-
gration. He was a sour thirty, with glasses and a flag pin.

John Alderdyce said, "At this point Walker's the only witness who can place Charlotte Sing in Detroit. The boy, Luis, is
being treated for narcotics poisoning; any statement from him
is bound to be spongy, given the hallucinogenic properties of
heroin and methadone. The Chinese is still on the table at Receiving Hospital, and we haven't been able to locate Ouida
Rogers. A neighbor heard her going out early this morning,
but she never showed up at work. We're questioning her employer, Eugenia Pappas, right now. Walker thinks she knows
something about the missing dope."

It was the first time I'd heard Ouida's last name. I figured she'd gone off somewhere to take stock. There's nothing like an overnight abduction to inspire you to reexamine your prospects.

"You're placing a great deal of faith in just his word. I understand your own forensics team has yet to raise physical evidence that Sing was ever in the manager's office or the equipment room at Tigers Stadium, much less this country. The assertion alone is a slap in the face to the officers who guard our borders."

Mary Ann Thaler spoke up. "That includes all three of us, metaphorically speaking; personally, I can take a little smack in the kisser if it means making good on a blunder. And you're forgetting the prints on that shipping carton. If Walker hadn't gotten her to touch it, he wouldn't have been invited to this meeting. That's just about the only thing he did last night that wasn't dumb."

"Thanks," I said. "The dummy's right here, by the way."

Here was a conference room in the MacNamara Federal Building, complete with a gold-fringed flag on a staff, portraits of Washington, Lincoln, and the current holder of their office, and upholstered chairs all around a walnut-veneer table you could play shuffleboard on. Thaler's office downstairs was too small to sew a button on a shirt without leaving the door open and Messarian said his was filled with boxes of files he hadn't unpacked yet. Apparently he wasn't the first bureaucrat to hold his post since the beginning of the year, or even the second. The job involved directing traffic between the FBI and the headquarters in Washington and the local Arab community, the largest outside the Middle East, and the burnout factor was high. I was pretty sure the boxed files were an excuse and wondered where they'd hidden the microphone.

"Assuming he's telling the truth and the carton wasn't planted to throw us off the trail," he said, "I don't understand how the Sing woman managed to slip away. Didn't you surround the building?"

"It takes more than the few minutes we had to surround one that size. The gates were designed to keep people out, not in, and there's a separate exit for club members and staff. Have you ever *been* to a ball game?" Alderdyce had little patience with feds, even the personable ones. He and Thaler had been on thin ice ever since she'd jumped the fence.

"Well, she won't get far. Her passport photo is at every airline counter and Customs checkpoint in the country. The borders are sealed tight."

We all three laughed. Messarian's ears reddened at the tips. It was a corner room, with windows looking out on Tigers Stadium and the narrow waterway separating the U.S. from the province of Ontario.

Alderdyce rose, his height and bulk tipping the balance of power in the room. The man from Washington seized upon this for diversion. "Where do you think you're going? This meeting isn't over."

"It is for me. The dragon lady's gone for sure. That makes her your problem now. Mine is tracking down those twenty kilos of goosed horse before they find their way into the veins of every junkie in the greater metropolitan area. That kind of quality in the hands of an experienced cooker could be in circulation for years." He left without having spoken to me or looked my way. I was going to have to deal away a lot of favors to make him forget I'd lied about not inviting Deputy Marshal Thaler to last night's tailgate party.

She was sore too, but right now she was angrier with the man at the head of the table. She rested a pair of unadorned wrists on the top. I wondered if the lack of jewelry and minimal cosmetics was a boardroom habit, as if she considered it a combat situation. "The reason these hypercriminals can waltz in and out of the U.S. with just a tip of the hat is we spend more time denying our failures than we do patching them up. When a citizen pitches in to help, we treat him like a suspect instead of an ally. If it weren't for Walker, we'd still be scratching our heads over just which fanatic with his forehead on the floor of some mosque was behind that shipment of poison. We thought it was to raise money for future terrorist plots. We never stopped to think it *was* the plot. We've hung out a reward of a million dollars for Madam Sing's capture and prosecution. So far no one's claimed it, but if the information he's given us leads that direction, we ought to cut him in."

"It seems grabby," I said. "I've already been paid twice for the same investigation."

"Shut up. You're not out of the woods. You're hiding a witness. You didn't take Chang out by yourself."

I shut up. I wasn't sure if a possible charge of vehicular assault wouldn't spoil Gale Kreski's defense in Guam. The law can be arbitrary even when the victim's in custody on suspicion of two counts of murder. Leaving Bud Lite out had kept me in an interview room at Detroit Homicide until an hour ago. I felt like a hair ball coughed up by a cat.

Messarian scowled. "How much does the press know?"

"You can't expect a blackout when you mount a joint-action armed offensive on a ballpark in the heart of the city. You need to call a press conference before the speculation gets out of hand."

"I wasn't asking for your advice. Deputy." He addressed me for the first time. "If you know what's good for you, you won't be giving interviews. Under the Patriot Act you can be booked on no charge at all and held indefinitely as a person of interest."

"That completes the set. I've already been threatened with arrest by the cops and the U.S. Marshals." I shrugged, not as eloquently as Luis Quincy Adams. "The paparazzi don't know me from Eleanor Roosevelt. I have to pay up front to get in the classifieds."

"Can we trust this person?"

"I don't trust *you*," Thaler said.

Out in the hall, she told me to walk and talk. She seemed always to be expected somewhere ten minutes ago. "Believe it or not, he's an improvement over the two that came before him. Washington doesn't assign you to Detroit as a reward for commendatory service. Why the double cross last night?"

"I thought you and John should kiss and make up. Ever see *The Parent Trap*?"

"Keep it up. I'm this close to feeding you to Messarian."

"I got scared. I had nothing to bargain with but ten empty boxes. I'd've rung in the Coast Guard if the place was closer to the water."

"You might have told me. We nearly fired on each other."

"You and John made it a condition to freeze each other out."

She rang for the service elevator. The media had been prowling the front lobby since the building opened. "So is Sing as crazy as they say?"

"Let's say she's consistent."

"I don't get this world-conquest jag. Do they ever stop to think what they'll do with it once they've got it?"

"She doesn't want the whole potato. She just wants to cut out the part she thinks is rotten."

"She can take her place in line just like everyone else."

The elevator came. We stepped aboard and she punched the button for the basement. The car was unfinished Sheetrock with a galvanized steel floor and smelled of forty-year-old cigars. The cables belched and shuddered and we started down hand under hand. "We're invited to sit in on Eugenia Pappas' interview," she said. "Detroit's claiming jurisdiction based on two murders and two kidnappings. The chief's wrangling it out with Justice."

"Can you tape it for me? I just spent four hours in that little room."

"I'll give Alderdyce your regrets."

"No one has that kind of time."

When we touched down, she pressed her thumb against the Doors Close button. "They don't bother to bug the service elevator. This is between us. Charlotte Sing in the picture means I'm just keeping the seat warm until a full marshal takes over, so we're two citizens talking. Who held your coat last night?"

"I said I was tired. I didn't say my brain went to sleep."

"I like to know how you work, for future reference. It doesn't leave this car." Her eyes were brown and level. "Consider it my price to recommend against your indefinite detention in a case involving national security."

"Why does that phrase always make my skin crawl?" I put my hands in my pockets. "He's busy staying out of the can himself. He's out on bail on a charge of open murder."

"Did he do it?"

"They say he used a gun. If he didn't bring one last night, he wouldn't have had one that day. The locals are starting to take interest in the victim's own personal security. He made enemies the way Quaker makes oats. It's federal," I said. "It happened in a U.S. protectorate."

I watched her as I said it. Her face showed no recognition. Well, it had been bumped below the fold by Saddam Hussein's hanging. She said, "I may be able to help. That stunt you two pulled could just as well be interpreted as civilian assistance in an official investigation. It would look good on the character side of his sheet."

"Why Santa Claus all of a sudden?"

"That clown upstairs thinks he can protect the Constitution by arresting everyone who looks at it crosswise. I think I can do as much letting a few of them go." She took her thumb off the button.

The basement looked like a scaled-down version of the government warehouse at the end of *Raiders of the Lost Ark,* stacked to the joists with cartons stenciled with number and letter codes, probably hard copies of files locked inside the computer system as backups in case the grid went down again. They'd cleared out the racks and iron maidens since Hoover's day. We walked up a loading ramp leading down from the alley behind the building. The sky hung low and leaden and there was an iron smell of snow in the air. November always comes right on schedule.

"I'll have to ask him," I said. "I'm already getting a reputation as a gossip."

"You and the Sphinx." She took the plastic ID tag from the lapel of her blazer and put it in her handbag. "While you're at it, tell him Bud Lite is a terrible name for a musician."

I slept away the rest of the morning despite pains in both legs and would have slept away the afternoon too if the telephone hadn't dragged me out of a fresh nightmare. I was in right field in Tigers Stadium and kept losing easy pop flies in the lights while the crowd screamed for my indefinite detention in a case involving national security.

I limped into the living room in my underwear and mumbled something into the receiver. It was John Alderdyce.

"I thought you might like to know we just kicked Eugenia Pappas," he said without greeting.

"How many lawyers did it take?"

"Just one, and if he'd had his way we'd still be holding her. Against his advice, she volunteered to submit to a lie detector test. She passed."

"A nut can beat those things."

"A psychopathic nut. They can tell bare-ass lies all day without a blip. She's a different kind of head case. Our department expert says she's telling the truth about that missing heroin; it was news to her. Now we're looking at her people, starting with that character in the warehouse."

"He doesn't know anything, including what's going on ten feet from his desk. He's just local color."

"I put in for a warrant to seize Eugenia's computer. Some-

one in her operation, maybe one of her charity workers, interrupted that shipment long enough to gut it. We picked up a
trace amount of dope from those converters you recovered. It
wasn't serendipity, a carton falling off a forklift and dumping
out its contents. They'd all been opened and resealed as neatly
as they came. Someone in a position to know what was inside
called the shots and someone else did the grunt work, for a
cut or wages. If we find one, we'll find the other."

"Any luck tracking down Ouida? She knows Eugenia's
operation better than Eugenia does."

"No. I was about to ask if you'd heard from her."

My doorbell rang just then. Life can be awfully tidy when
it wants to be.

THIRTY

It rang again while I was putting on a robe, followed by knocking as I strode to the door. I'd left the Luger in the office and the .38 in the car, but it was the middle of the day, and people like Madam Sing belonged to the night.

Ouida looked like Hollywood's idea of a refugee from the Eastern Bloc. She had on a long dark cloth coat buttoned up to her chin, dark glasses, and a scarf tied over the brilliant cranberry of her hair. A leather bag the size of an overnight case hung from a strap on her shoulder. "Please, can you let me in quickly?" She was out of breath.

I stepped aside and she fled across the threshold. I closed the door while she drew off the glasses. Her eyes were scrubbed free of last night's smeared makeup. Without it she looked twelve years old. They lit on the robe. "I didn't mean to wake you."

"I was up. Have you slept?"

"I tried. I never thanked you for last night. You saved my life."

"Maybe not. Lives don't mean much to Charlotte Sing, but she doesn't kill just for fun."

"I don't suppose they've found her?"

I shook my head. "They're looking for you, too, but I guess you know that. Hardly anyone dresses like Bette Davis around here."

"I was afraid they would be, that's why I left home. I—I need a few days to myself before facing their questions. These past twenty-four hours have been a horror."

"There's a cure for that."

I went into the kitchen, dumped ice into two squat mismatched glasses, filled the rest with spirits, and carried them with the bottle on a tray into the living room. She'd shaken her hair loose from the scarf and was sitting in the armchair with her coat off and spread behind her, holding the leather bag in her lap. I put the tray on the coffee table, handed her a glass, and sat down opposite her on the sofa with mine.

"You have a lot of books," she said. "I didn't figure you for a reading man."

"I've been taking lessons."

"I noticed you're limping. Did that Chang creature hurt you badly?"

"Not as bad as the others. He ran into some bad luck himself. I guess he didn't read his fortune cookie."

"The news reports are all garbled. Nobody seems to know what's going on."

"Where'd you go after you left the house?"

"A motel. I paid cash and used a false name, but I suppose that wasn't original. I heard some men asking the clerk about check-ins when I came out of my room to get a bottle of water from the machine. I went out by the side stairs."

"Is that all your luggage?"

She glanced down at the bag, her fingers tightening on it. "Just some things for a couple of days. Could you put me up? I can pay you for your trouble."

"I bet you can. Drink your drink. It eats through the glass if you let it sit."

"Should we toast something?"

"Only after six. This time of day it's medicine."

We drank. She made the face women make and leaned forward to set her glass on the tray. She lifted the flap on her bag, reached inside, and laid a bank envelope on my side of the table. "I hope it's enough."

I put down my drink and picked up the envelope. There were ten bills inside, all the same denomination. Ben Franklin always looks as if he came fresh from a night's sleep. He doesn't knock around as much as the others. I said, "I hope you're okay with basic cable."

"I'll try not to be too much trouble. You won't know I'm here. On the other hand, if you'd rather you did, that's okay." A wicked smile pulled at the corners of her lips. Naughty child.

"I'll have to charge you extra for that." I slid the envelope into a robe pocket, lifted my glass, and sat back.

Patches of red showed on her cheeks, as if I'd slapped her. "I take back what I said last night. I didn't misjudge you at all."

"I got up on the wrong side of bed a week ago and I haven't gotten over it yet. This all started when I ran out of coffee. A cop I'm friendly with, who happened to be standing at the end of the coffee aisle, put me on to a job, simple recovery work that ought to have meant nothing more than a little horse trading with a local fence and three days' pay for six-teen hours' work. I crashed a car, ran a marathon, got threat-ened with arrest for treason, took a couple of hits, and learned way more than I wanted to know about gangs in Red China. As pleasant as it sounds, getting laid just isn't enough. Nei-ther is a grand."

"It's all I can spare. Eugenia doesn't pay me much."

"You can get more. You're her good right hand."

"I doubt I still am. I haven't reported for work in two days." What I'd said seemed to dawn on her then. "Are you suggest-ing I embezzle from her?"

"Don't act like it's a new idea."

She saw me looking at the bag and closed both hands on it. The whiteness faded from the knuckles slowly, an effort of will. "I'm sure I need that drink, but I can get it down better with a glass of water. I'm dehydrated. I never got that bottle from the vending machine."

I went back into the kitchen and filled a tumbler from the tap. When I returned, I looked at the small brushed-steel semi-automatic pistol she was holding. "You've been on quite the spending spree," I said.

"It didn't cost me a cent. Eugenia will never miss it. I found it in a drawer full of scarves and handkerchiefs she's never worn. Nick was no better than most men when it comes to giving gifts their wives can use."

"You should've used it on Chang."

"I kept it at home. I couldn't afford to get caught carrying an unregistered gun. I'm an amateur. I didn't want to make an amateur's mistake."

"You've got millions of dollars in heroin in that bag. I'd

say you're a pro. Where's the rest of it? That bag wouldn't hold forty-plus pounds."

She hesitated. "I had to split it with someone else. Just when did you arrive at that conclusion?"

"You're even starting to sound like Charlotte Sing. I had my suspicions when you weren't home when the cops came calling. The thousand dollars was a stronger indication; this house isn't the MGM Grand. It was the gun that cinched it. I'm a little slow on the uptake today. Normally I have a theory in place by the time the artillery comes out. How'd you manage it?"

"Delegated responsibilities. I told you the day we met I handle all of Eugene's correspondence. She prefers to play the role of the benefactress in the ivory tower and leave the details to the peasants. The world's run by clerks and secretaries. I knew there had to be more to a simple shipment of converter boxes than a *Three's Company* marathon; yours wasn't the only inquiry. At the time I'd never heard of Madam Sing—really, do people call her that?—but as of the day before yesterday I knew something more was behind them than just a search for stolen merchandise. When they showed up in the system, I put someone on them. Eugenia's just a name on a paycheck for most of the people who work for her. They deal with me on a day-to-day basis. The rest was a simple business transaction."

"It got a little more complicated when Sing had you snatched."

"I admit I didn't give enough thought to the ruthlessness of the drug business. I'm an underpaid flunky. That worked for me all the time she had me tied to a chair. All I had to do was beg her for mercy. I was sincere about that—up to a point. I wasn't faking last night; I was scared as hell the whole time she had me, her and that killer she hired. If she'd once pressed me about that heroin, I'd have spilled the whole thing. When she didn't, I knew there were worse things than being tied to a chair. Going on the way I had, for instance."

"She's not as smart as she's made out to be," I said. "She was a slave before she was a billionaire. She took advantage of the fact that she was invisible in order to get where she got. She inherited the mistakes that made her what she is. Who'd you recruit for the grunt work? Those hands never drew a staple from a shipping carton."

"Just another version of myself, a little lower on the scale. I cut him in for half; I'd tried for less, but I tipped my hand. I said I'm an amateur. Hold still!" The gun came up, shaking a little. The tremor did nothing for my confidence; guns go off in unsteady hands more often than not. I paused with my hand in my robe pocket.

"Just my cigarettes and matches. I like to have something in my hands when I'm at gunpoint."

"You can smoke when you're back on the way to the American side. You're taking me to Canada."

"Now you're back to amateur. That's just what they're expecting."

"If I am a suspect, they'll be looking for a woman traveling alone, under a passport made out to Ouida Rogers. I have one; Eugenia's business takes me across the border three or four times a year. I had the photo transferred to another name. That's what's taken me all this time. Having contact with all of Eugenia's people means I have contact with all of Nick's. Did you know the U.S. passport is easier to forge than a Michigan driver's license? I didn't, until after I'd parted with another thousand. I hope yours is up to date." She showed uncertainty for the first time. It had been there right along, below the surface. Her finger tightened on the trigger.

"Shooting me won't get you there any faster. I've got a copy of my application. That's all I need for now."

"Get it, and get dressed. When they ask you your reason for visiting Canada, tell them you and your fiancée are going to the casino in Windsor. They like that. Business has fallen off since they made them legal here."

"Suppose we make it? Michigan doesn't have the death penalty. Ottawa won't block extradition."

"You let me worry about that. I've got all the traveling papers I need." She patted her bag.

I was running out of stalls, but just then a squawking noise drew her attention to the table beside the armchair. It was the signal that the telephone was off the hook and the party on the other end had hung up.

I said, "I was talking to the cops when you came to the door. I guess I didn't get it all the way back on the cradle." As I spoke I scooped the envelope out of my pocket and dashed the bills in her face.

She fired, but I was moving by then, and the flutter of hundred-dollar bills threw off her aim. A police forensics expert made the hole in the ceiling worse digging out the slug. I let my momentum carry us both over backwards, chair and all, and had my foot on the wrist of her gun arm when the first prowl car swirled into the driveway.

The jury went easy on Ouida. She gave up her partner, who surrendered to Narcotics officers with ten kilos of heroin stashed under the bed in his apartment in Sterling Heights, and got five to ten. She'll probably draw probation on appeal as a first offender. Shau Win Chang got tourist-class passage to Beijing, handcuffed to Deputy U.S. Marshal Mary Ann Thaler, and the chance to preboard on a disability; soldiers greeted him when he disembarked. Charlotte Sing got another million on the reward for her arrest and conviction and an hour on *Dateline*. I got a picture postcard of the Great Wall signed by Thaler. Her offer to bear witness to Gale Kreski's character was declined when the U.S. district court dismissed all charges against him on the evidence of a confession by a member of Winfield's personal bodyguard; one of the record producer's staff thought he'd been cheated out of money he'd helped cheat from clients, and had claimed his due by right of vendetta. Kreski went on to an early vote-off on *American Idol*, but earned enough to buy back his piano. I'm invited to celebrate the event, but I haven't RSVPed. My one good suit is still awaiting repair at the tailor's.

The Sing woman wakes me up nights. The thought of evil without abstraction always has, but proof that it exists and is walking around somewhere in broad daylight is like a triple shot of No-Doz. It makes me get up and double-check all my locks.

Luis Quincy Adams occupies nearly as much of my thinking time. When I went to visit him at Detroit Receiving Hospital, the nurse at the station told me he'd released himself without leaving a billing address. A subpoena was issued for his testimony to a grand jury investigating the latest instance of domestic terrorism, but no one could run fast enough to serve it. I've given up watching ESPN for news from Mexico City; Argentina continues to table petitions to reinstate bullfighting in its jurisdiction. The bulls there can rest easy for a while, but I'm not so sure about Pamplona.

AUTHOR'S NOTE

When *Infernal Angels*—the twenty-first novel to feature Amos Walker—appears, it will mark thirty years in which Walker will have occupied some small part of the world's fabric.

In the cosmic scheme of things, the time is hardly vast, but it represents more years than I'd lived when I created the character in 1980. I was twenty-eight, Walker (as I recall) thirty-two; at this writing I'm fifty-five, and when last recorded, Walker was somewhere in his forties. Someone once said that heroes age on a sliding scale, but having established him as a veteran of the Vietnamese War, I will at some point have to acknowledge that he's passed the half-century mark.

But letting him age has advantages. I'm a rough old cob of a god and have put him through plenty. To do it all over again, without asking him to face the additional challenges of growing older and the inevitable effect of those ordeals on a middle-aged body, would be to risk monotony, not to mention incredulity. ("In the pursuit of my profession I'd been shot, beaten, coldcocked, drugged, and threatened with death. . . . It would be a good joke on a lot of bad people if it was a heart episode that took me.") I put a bullet through his thigh in *Nicotine Kiss* and three books later he's still limping; Vicodin has joined his daily regimen of cigarettes and Scotch. He's never been Superman. He's smart enough to fill in the blanks when they begin to form a pattern, but he's not a savant. He can hold his own in a fight, but he sometimes loses, and more often lately than when he was in his prime. He has enough courage to defy ordinary odds and enough caution to hold back when they're extraordinary. Even Superman has his Kryptonite, or he'd be insufferable. If Walker's courage, strength, and intelligence are to be tested further, I can't think of an opponent more formidable than time itself.

The years have sped. His birth seems so recent, yet Jimmy Carter was president, the United States was being held hostage in Iran, there was no Indiana Jones, no Madonna, no Internet. Cell phones were science fiction, "rap" meant *talk*, and AIDS was an obscure African disease attributed to eating monkey meat. In Detroit, Walker's main port of call, there was still hope that the local auto industry would turn around and reverse the damages caused by the 1967 race riot and the Murder City years of the 1970s. Who'd have thought that three decades later the picture would still be bleak? But bad times for cities are fodder for crime fiction, and Walker will never be stumped for an opportunity to risk everything for small-*j* justice.

His greatest challenge, however, came not in Detroit, but from New York City. At the beginning of the 1990s, a legal dispute with a publisher forced me to place the character on a seven-year hiatus from books. Although I managed to keep him alive in short stories placed with *Ellery Queen's Mys-*

tery Magazine, Alfred Hitchcock's Mystery Magazine, New Black Mask, and a number of anthologies, the readership wasn't precisely the same, and I was afraid he'd be forgotten. But when I reintroduced him to novels with *Never Street* in 1997, the reception was strong enough to continue the series through today.

It would be ignorant as well as arrogant to claim more than my part for this longevity, particularly in view of the fact that so many excellent series that were created by other authors at the same time have perished. Ruth Hapgood launched Amos Walker when she bought *Motor City Blue* for Houghton Mifflin, James Frenkel of Tom Doherty Associates edited the book you're holding as well as *Poison Blonde, Retro, Nicotine Kiss, American Detective,* and *The Left-Handed Dollar,* Bill Malloy of the Mysterious Press returned Walker to the bookstalls after his long holiday, the late Cathleen Jordan edited Walker stories for *Alfred Hitchcock's Mystery Magazine,* where her successor, Linda Landrigan, continues the tradition, and Janet Hutchings brought him (and his creator) to *Ellery Queen's Mystery Magazine* for the first time. The relationship between writers and copy editors is often adversarial and too frequently contentious, but that has never been the case between me and, first, Lois Randall, then MaryAnn Johanson, whose skill and hard work have kept Mary Ann Thaler's brown eyes from turning blue from book to book (I doubt their common Christian name is a factor), as well as many other embarrassments from coming to light.

Louisa Rudeen helmed the Fawcett Books reissues of the first ten titles in mass-market paperback, widely distributing them in stylish packages. At Brilliance Corporation, Eileen Hutton brought Amos Walker to audio for the first time. My association with all the editors I've worked with on the series has run in direct opposition to the old aphorism that an editor is never your friend.

From 2000 through 2004, the late Byron Preiss returned the early Walkers to print through his I-Books trade paperback line, introducing the character to a new generation and the twenty-first century.

Supporters who have passed on are too many, and never forgotten. In addition to Cathleen Jordan and Byron Preiss they include Ray and Barbara Puechner, my first literary agents; former Detroiter Phil Thomas, longtime reviewer with the Associated Press and an early Walker booster; Neal Shine, legendary editor-in-chief of the *Detroit Free Press*; and Professor Curtis Stadtfeld, my mentor at Eastern Michigan University and for many years afterward. Amos Walker survives in part because they lived.

I'm deeply grateful to Millie Puechner and Dominick Abel, whose performance and succor have blasted the stereotype of the venal literary agent to bits.

Readers who have embraced the series from Eight Mile Road to the Ginza Strip are never far from my thoughts. Their patience and loyalty have been fixtures as dependable as Walker's 1970 Cutlass.

Finally, I give thanks to my wife, Deborah Morgan, who has sacrificed time from her own writing career to promote the Walker books as well as the rest of my work, with great success. She's a better man than us both.

ABOUT THE AUTHOR

Loren D. Estleman has written more than sixty novels. He has netted four Shamus Awards for detective fiction, five Spur Awards for Western fiction, and three Western Heritage Awards, among his many professional honors. *Infernal Angels* is the twenty-first Amos Walker mystery. He lives with his wife, author Deborah Morgan, in Michigan.